In all her nineteen years there had been nothing that had taught her how to behave when faced with a man who falsely believed they were soon to be wed, and who might fall into a fatal illness if he learned the truth. She should be discreet. She should withdraw.

Instead, she closed her eyes. She felt his breath on her cheek. Then his mouth touched hers gently; her lips parted in a silent gasp of surprise.

He dragged his lips across hers again, and again, until the contours of her mouth altered, swelling and molding to the supple shape of his. This pulsing sweetness was a new world for Mary, black shot with flashes of gold and red, bursting through her blood like sparks of fire. . . .

Also by Leslie Lynn
Published by Fawcett Books:

RAKE'S REDEMPTION
SCANDAL'S CHILD
A SOLDIER'S HEART

THE DUKE'S DECEIT

Leslie Lynn

FAWCETT CREST · NEW YORK

To Barbara Dicks for her support and encouragement

A Fawcett Crest Book
Published by Ballantine Books
Copyright © 1993 by Elaine Sima and Sherrill Bodine

Library of Congress Catalog Card Number: 92-97253

ISBN 0-449-21969-0

Manufactured in the United States of America

First Edition: April 1993

Prologue

"Avalon, have you heard but *one* word I've spoken to you?"

Richard, Duke of Avalon, was struck by two very disparate emotions as he stared down into the perfect oval that was his fiancée's face.

The first evoked a sharp pain in the region of his heart. Even after eighteen months the memory of his father's death could wash over him in a numbing wave of grief. Always, he missed that source of strength and gentle wisdom. He would never be truly comfortable as "Your Grace", instead of as the plain Marquis of Longford.

The second was stinging self-mockery as he recalled the words his delightful sister-in-law, Serena, had once flung at him. "It is my fondest wish that when your tiny heart is finally given, the lady crumbles it to dust." There was no danger that his betrothed could perform such a feat for she did not now, nor would she ever, possess his heart.

"Avalon, don't you dare to give me that mocking smile in the very midst of Lady Norton's ball!" His betrothed forgot herself so far as to stomp her slippered foot. As usual, Lady Arabella Hampton's beauty was marred by a pout. His cronies, and the haut monde in general, found this habit charming.

After all, such an incomparable should expect to have the world and all at her feet.

But he was beginning to find it irritating.

"Bella, if you stomp your slipper again, the entire room will know we are feuding," he drawled, lowering his lids to mere slits.

She fanned herself heatedly with a delicate yellow bit of whimsy painted with blue forget-me-nots.

"No one heard me." Thrusting up her chin she glared at him. "Everyone else is enjoying themselves! But you have not danced with me once this evening!"

Shrugging, he turned away to gaze lazily at the whirling mass in the ballroom. Candlelight caught the blaze of jewels at throats, earlobes, and wrists, sending twinkling light to bounce against the dim walls. The press of bodies was so great it was difficult to determine where one person ended and the other began. There was not one tiny space free.

This frantic effort had always bored him. But duty was duty, and could not be ignored, now that he was the duke. So against his mother's wishes, and his own inclination, he had thrown himself into the social season, determined to find a wife. The succession must be secured. And at five-and-thirty it was time he was setting up his nursery. After all, his brother had wed just such a chit, and it had turned into quite a match—she was a woman to reckon with.

He relented slightly. "If you're bored, my dear, by all means let us take our leave," he teased, preparing to do the pretty and escort her in the next waltz.

"Yes, let us depart at once!" she snapped back.

At last she had surprised him. He gave a bark of genuine laughter. "Odds fish, Bella! I've never known you to leave a squeeze like this before dawn."

"Well, you have managed to give me a headache," she pouted. "I hope you're pleased with yourself!" With her chin thrust to the ceiling, she abandoned him to cross the room, a trail of eyes following her.

Dutifully, he followed in her wake.

Her cheeks flushed, she bade Lady Norton farewell. Standing just so as to catch the candlelight gleaming in her golden curls, she appeared every inch a future duchess. At first her pets and starts had been amusing; now, he was beginning to wonder if there was aught beneath. He was in too deep, no matter his decision. A betrothal was a pledge that he could never break.

Smiling and nodding graciously to the crowd gathered at the curb, Arabella descended the front steps. He was about to reassure himself about his choice—she would play the role of duchess to the nines—when she spoiled the picture by turning to hiss at him.

"I hope at the Duchess of Cumberland's Grand Ball you are more the thing, Avalon."

He waited until they were in the coach before answering. In truth, the idea came to him at just that moment. "I shan't be there, my dear."

"Whatever do you mean?" There was nothing ducal about the shriek she uttered, plainly audible to all gathered about the barouche, whose top had been collapsed due to the unseasonably fine weather they were experiencing.

"I plan to leave for Scotland tomorrow. There is

a professor of philosophy at the University of Edinburgh I've long been interested in meeting." Warming to this new idea he flicked the tip of her nose with one finger. "Don't fret, Bella, I'll return before the wedding."

"Before the wedding!" she gasped, both hands fluttering to her heaving bosom. "What of the Duchess of Cumberland's? It is the most important event of the season."

"Surely not?" He couldn't resist lifting his eyebrow in disdain.

"Just because we are betrothed does not mean you can ignore me, my lord." Her voice rose with each word.

"Not even *I* can get to Edinburgh and back within a fortnight, Bella. Even on my wildest stallion." Eager to be on his way, he tapped the coachman's arm. "No doubt one of your court will be happy to stand in my place."

Unaccountably the coach remained in place, directly before the entrance and under the *torchères*.

"If you do not escort me to the Duchess of Cumberland's Grand Ball, I shall cry off from this marriage. Do you hear me?" She issued her challenge in her most formidable tone, no doubt cultivated to bring the most erring of suitors into line.

"Not only do I hear you," he drawled sarcastically, "but so does half the ton."

Her pale blue eyes widened in horror as she suddenly realized that they were surrounded by dozens of party goers standing at shocked attention. Casting him a look of pure loathing, she flung herself into the farthest corner of the carriage and snapped open her fan.

4

Richard's low growl, "James!" brought the coachman to his senses and they began to roll forward.

More than a few members of the ton fell back, clearing a path before the long stare from his unreadable eyes. Ignoring their interested faces, he sprawled at ease until they reached the near corner and turned it.

He leaned forward again and touched James's shoulder. "Pull up here. Take the young lady home safely, James. I'll walk to Avalon House." He turned to Arabella and took one gloved hand into his own. "Good evening, Bella," he declared evenly, "I'll see you on my return. And, of course, I'll abide by any decisions you have made."

He looked her full in the face and recognized the moment when she acknowledged defeat. Really he should feel some remorse at having put her so neatly in her place. Instead he felt only relief. He strolled off, his steps buoyed by a new energy. At last! The opportunity to escape this endless tedium. He'd find a place where men thought of something besides the fold of their cravats or the toss of the dice. It was the sanest move he'd made in months, even if he must endure another of Bella's famous snits.

Richard went directly to his wing of the house and roused his valet to inform him that he must be packed and on the road to Scotland by dawn. Crowley did not question such a rash decision; he merely arched his bushy gray brows and inquired if His Grace would be traveling with the baggage coaches.

"Goodness no!" He was caught up with anticipation, the first real excitement he'd felt since the battle of Waterloo two years before, when delivering the Duke of Wellington's communiqués to his commanders had given him a true sense of purpose. He wanted the fresh bracing air of the country on his face and the feel of powerful horseflesh beneath him. "I'm going ahead on Wildfire. Don't look for me until you get to the Caladonia in Edinburgh."

He pulled on his riding clothes. Now that he had decided, nothing would hinder his departure. But before he could go he had to stop in the library. He flung a glass of port down his throat and then sat at the dark walnut desk to pen a note to his mother. He wouldn't wake her at this unseemly hour.

As if the thought had conjured her up, his mother stood before him. A scent of roses filled the air; her white hair was braided in one long plait, pulled tightly back from a face still unbelievably lovely, even in age, dominated by the dark flashing eyes which were her legacy to all her children.

"I understand you are leaving for Scotland at dawn. And if you don't return within a fortnight Arabella is crying off."

His mother's calm pronouncement hardly fazed him. However she did it, he'd never understand, but she always knew everything.

"The gossip mill grinds even at this hour!" He stepped forward to kiss her cheek. "I don't doubt you know what will happen in the next day, not to mention two hours ago."

"No matter, dearest one. I understand you must go. What will transpire will no doubt be for the best."

"You wanted this union, Mother," he said softly, for he understood her best of all her children.

"It was spoken of long ago, before I knew who and what you would be; but there was never a constraint on you, Richard." She crossed to the bookcase and, searching its shelves, finally located a dark leather-bound volume. Pulling it from its place she put it in his hands. "You go on a great journey."

"Mother, I . . ."

Lovingly cupping his chin with her graceful fingers, she gazed solemnly up into his face. "I wonder, do you know what you seek?"

Identical chocolate eyes met, and hers held his in a long searching look. It was impossible now, just as it had always been, to tell her less than the truth.

"No. But I shall know when I find it. Then, never fear, I shall return to do my duty."

Chapter 1

Mary Masterton sat bolt upright in her narrow bed and stared around the small slope-ceilinged room. For a moment her eyes wouldn't focus. Blinking rapidly, she tried to clear her vision. Slowly shadows began to take familiar shapes. She breathed a sigh of relief. Nothing stirred. Everything was neatly in place: the low cherry-wood chest with her silver brush and comb on its highly polished top, and next to it the curved rocking chair which had once been her mother's; all familiar, dear in the memories they evoked.

Then what had awakened her? She settled the covers about her, preparing to lie back down. Her long, heavy hair had come undone from its neat plait, and she smoothed the tendrils away from her face as she glanced toward her favorite dreaming place, the cushioned window seat. The first fingers of dawn's light always touched that window, turning it the soft pink of Lottie's beloved roses.

Odd. This morning the sunlight was fiery in color and the glass glowed red-gold.

Intrigued, she flung back the coverlet and padded across the cool wood floor. She curled up on the window seat and pressed her nose to the glass.

Her heart nearly burst from her chest. Fire!

Flames shot from behind the stable, then fell to the roof. Flowing along the eaves like a scarlet blanket, they spread down the walls as she watched.

The horses!

"Uncle Ian!" she screamed, wrenching open her bedroom door. "Uncle Ian, the stable is on fire!" she shouted through his door, giving the wood a hard slap with her flat palm as she flew past.

She ran out into the yard and toward the stable. Gray smoke choked her but she ran into it, all feelings deadened except one: the need to save her horses.

She pulled the stable door open and heat slammed into her, nearly knocking her over with its force.

"It's all right! I'm here!" she tried to shout over the wild cries of the horses.

The smoke blinded her, but she knew the stable. Lara and Beauty were to her left, Lightning and Black to her right. The other mares were penned at the back.

She turned to the left, feeling along the wood until she reached Beauty's stall. Grabbing a halter, she tangled her fingers in the mare's mane and forced her to submit to the lead. Beauty didn't want to leave the safety of her stall. It took all of Mary's strength to pull her forward.

"Mary! Get out, girl!" Uncle Ian shouted, running toward her with his white nightshirt flapping out of hastily pulled-on trousers.

"Take Beauty!" She thrust the mare's lead into his hands and spun on the balls of her feet to dash back.

She heard him cursing behind her. A moment later he was beside her.

"Get the Black! I'll go to Lara!" she commanded.

Lara rolled her eyes in terror, and Mary quieted her, laying a hand against the chestnut mane. "Lara, girl, I'm here," she soothed through her aching throat. Although the mare's eyes were still wild, she dropped her head in recognition.

Suddenly the hayloft above her burst into flame. Heat seared her skin, the hot air almost impossible to take into her lungs. She found the water bucket and dashed some into her face. She must hurry!

She grabbed Lara's mane and pulled herself up bareback. Mary tightened her bare thighs around the mare's trembling flesh, forcing her to respond. Her throat was too tight and dry to speak, but she leaned forward over the chestnut neck, making clucking sounds and encouraging Lara out of the stable.

The moment she was free of the stable door she slid off the mare's back. "Freedom," she choked, and slapped Lara's rump hard, hoping she would run to the far field where she pastured.

Her eyes watered so from the painful burning smoke that she pressed them closed momentarily to gain an instant of relief. Coughing, she stumbled into the yard blindly. Hearing Lottie's cries of panic, she opened her lids.

Directly ahead of her, the black silhouette of a man on horseback wavered through the gray smoke billowing through the yard.

He leapt down and ran toward her. "How many horses are left in there?"

His voice commanded, forcing her out of her state of shock.

Uncle Ian emerged from the smoke leading a recalcitrant Black, who minced back two steps for every pace forward.

"Seven!" she shouted. "Six are penned together. I'll take care of Lightning!"

She turned, running back into the blazing stable. The stranger raced beside her.

"Where are they?" he shouted, and she pointed to the back of the stable, where flames engulfed the wooden beams.

He disappeared into the black smoke as Mary ducked a piece of flaming wood, fear pounding through her with such force that for an instant she couldn't move. The next moment a crash beside her spurred her forward. There wasn't much time left.

Lightning was plunging wildly, kicking against the wooden slats of his stall. No matter what she tried, he wouldn't let her get a lead on him. The heat scorched her skin, and breathing was like drinking flames. Dizzy from holding her breath, Mary fell to her knees, knocking against Lightning's water bucket. In one last desperate lunge she threw the water at the horse, startling him and drenching herself. Revived momentarily, she grabbed an old blanket and threw it over his head to blind him. With the last of her strength she grabbed a handful of mane and pulled.

She sobbed as, miraculously, he moved.

"I'm here, Lightning, that's a good boy," she croaked, leading him into the yard.

Ian ran past her.

"Mary, don't go back in there! I can't handle these horses alone," Lottie sobbed, holding Beauty and Black with trembling hands.

Mary nodded, knowing Lottie hardly knew one end of a horse from the other, and gently took the other reins. "It will be all right, Lottie. We must lead them over here to the far paddock. Have you seen Lara?"

Her voice was raspy and her throat ached, but it didn't matter any more than her bleeding and burned bare limbs mattered. They were saving the horses.

"Lottie, shut them in here," she said gently. "I've got to get back for the other horses."

The entire roof of the stable burned a bright red glow against the dawn light. She swayed to a stop, watching the flames destroy her father's dream. Tears streamed down her cheeks but she clenched her fists, determined to save the rest of her precious stock.

Suddenly the stranger burst through the doorway with two of the young mares. "Take them!"

He thrust the reins into her hands. Before she could stop him he was gone, dashing past Ian as he came through with two more mares.

Even though reaction was setting in, making every movement a struggle to perform without shaking, she quickly led the horses to the paddock, where Lottie leaned wearily against the gate.

Rolling tears left streaks of white on her smoke-grimed cheeks, but Lottie managed a quaking smile. "We're going to save them all, aren't we Mary?"

"Yes. Just two more." She was horrified to hear the sob in her voice. "Just two more and everyone will be safe."

Remembering the stranger, she whirled, running back to help him.

The wind fed the fire, sending it in high bright fingers of russet toward the dawn sun. Suddenly a gust blew the billowing black smoke away from the entrance. Mary saw the stranger leading out the last two horses.

He must have heard the ominous creaking noise at the same instant she did, for she saw him slap the rumps of both horses, sending them racing away toward her.

But he didn't escape. The edge of the falling lintel beam caught the back of his head.

A scream of horror ripped from her aching throat. As he tumbled forward she rushed to help him, sidestepping the bolting horses.

He fell just inside the ruined stable. A blazing timber lay across one hessian. She pushed it away, singeing her fingers.

With both hands she grabbed under his arms to pull him out to the yard. His weight fought her strength. Giving one wrenching sob, she dug her feet firmly into the dirt and pulled even harder. She had to get him to safety! The stable was completely engulfed, the back wall fallen in. Her burned feet and bruised fingers were numb and helpless against his unresponsive form.

"Give way, Mary, my girl," Uncle Ian spoke suddenly from behind her.

Tears of relief choked her as Ian took the burden from her hands. The stranger was taller than her uncle, but Ian possessed a strength belied by his small stature.

With a grunt, he hefted the stranger over his shoulder. "Which room, Mary girl?"

"Mine."

She ran ahead to straighten the covers and plump her feather pillow. By the time Ian entered with the stranger hanging limply over his shoulder, she was already considering what to do to help this knight-errant.

Her horses were all safe. It was a miracle, and they'd never have done it without him!

"Careful with the poor soul," Lottie fussed, following Ian in.

The stranger dwarfed her small bed. His long limbs hung over the end where Ian knelt to pull off his boots. She looked at him, wondering who he was. Why had he been riding down the lane so early in the morning?

He moaned and turned his head as his second boot came off. Blood oozed through his dark wavy hair onto the white cotton pillow cover. His face was caked with grime from the thick smoke.

She reached for the linen cloth hanging beside her washstand and dipped it into the bowl. Carefully she cleaned his face.

"Lottie, please fetch some lint so we can wrap his head," she said without stopping her task. The cloth smoothed his forehead, cleaning bits of ash out of his dark eyebrows. She rinsed it in the bowl, then softly ran it over his high cheekbones and into the deep grooves that ran from either side of his nose.

It was a strong face, she decided, the face of one used to getting his own way. For some inexplicable reason, perhaps reaction to everything that had happened in the last hour, her fingers trembled slightly as she pressed the cloth to his firm lips.

He murmured something unintelligible and turned his face into her hand. A tremor ran through her. He was so helpless, and all because he'd helped her!

Lottie returned, and together they wound a

length of lint around his head to stay the blood from the wound.

"We've stopped the bleeding, but he must have a doctor. Uncle Ian, go for Dr. McAlister while I make him more comfortable," she commanded, her fingers already fumbling with his ruined cravat.

Her uncle grabbed her wrist in an iron grip. "You're not about to undress him yourself. You may be forgettin' who you are, my girl, but I am not. Lottie, fetch me that salve from the oak chest." Ian threw the words over his shoulder, his steady eyes challenging Mary.

She shook free of his grasp. "Uncle Ian, don't be absurd! I am nineteen and not about to swoon at the sight of a naked chest. This poor man needs our help!"

"And that he'll be gettin'," Ian declared, his usually merry mouth a hard straight slash in his narrow flushed face. "Ah, Lottie, thank'ee lass."

Handing the salve to Ian, Lottie cast Mary an understanding glance from red-rimmed eyes. She responded with her most pleading look, but Lottie merely shook her head. There would be no help from that quarter.

"What do you expect me to do? Pace the hallway wringing my hands like the veriest miss while you attend to his needs?"

Already tackling the ruined lawn shirt, her uncle ignored her. He could be just as stubborn as she.

"Mary, Ian's right." Lottie placed one plump hand on Mary's shoulder, urging her up from the bed. "Come away now. You should be after checking your horse and making sure the others are all right. There's much to be done elsewhere. It's not proper for you to be here."

Knowing how hard Lottie always strived to do "the proper," Mary relented. "I shall do as you ask, Lottie. But when I return I insist on helping!"

Making her way down the narrow stairs, she felt the burns on her calves and feet begin to blister, making it difficult to walk without a limp. Biting her lip against the pain, she moved out into the yard.

The stable was gone. All that remained was a grotesque ruin of blackened timbers that smoldered and occasionally spit out a burst of red sparks. Mary was grateful the wind had died so there was no threat to the house.

She could see her horses, huddled together at the far side of the paddock, Lara nosing Beauty from outside the fence. But the stranger's stallion stood exactly where he had been left. Running a palm along his black glossy neck, she marveled at his lines. He was the finest Arabian she'd ever seen. If she had such a magnificent stud, all her problems would be over.

The Moroccan leather of the saddlebag only reinforced what she already suspected; her unknown hero was someone of quality. The bag yielded two fresh lawn shirts and five cravats. When she lifted out his personal linen, her cheeks burned with embarrassment. She quickly stuffed them back and pulled out a slim leather-bound volume.

On the inside cover was a clue to his identity. "To my son, Richard. With love, Mother."

Richard. That was all. That, and the trappings of wealth.

Perhaps he came from the life her mother had abandoned so long ago. It was a dream world of princes and queens, of elaborate balls and stately homes and beautiful flowing gowns. Mary's head was full of the stories her mother had told of her life before she'd married John Masterton and come to live at the Scottish border. She never regretted a moment of that life, she'd insisted, content with her husband and their small horse farm.

After the terrible winter when her parents died, Mary had briefly dreamed of going to London and tasting that life. But it was a world that was forever closed to her, regardless of Uncle Ian's protestations. According to the solicitor, her grandfather wanted nothing to do with her. He would only continue to pay the tiny stipend Mary's mother had received from her mother if she stayed away from society and didn't disgrace him.

Clasping the book to the thin cotton bodice of her ruined night robe, Mary surveyed her world, the only world she had ever known, or was likely to know.

At least the snug two-story cottage where she had been born was unharmed. Lottie's roses still climbed one wall, spangling the whitewash with splashes of pink. The reek of smoke swirled around her, but she lifted her chin, refusing to give in to despair. This was her father's legacy to her: the horses and this small piece of land. No one could or would take it away from her.

And now she had a stranger to thank for that. If he hadn't helped . . . She couldn't bear to think of it!

She grabbed the reins of Richard's horse; at first he wouldn't move, but Mary had a way with animals. She cooed softly into his ear as she coaxed him into a smaller ring next to her own horses. She called to Lara and let her into the paddock so she would be safe.

Limping slightly, she went about her chores, taking the tack off the stranger's horse and feeding and watering all the animals. All the while she refused to look at the smoldering heap that had once been the stable.

After she finished, she picked up the book and went back into the house. Uncle Ian was in the kitchen, putting salve on his own burns.

"Done the best we can, Mary girl. I'll be off to fetch Dr. McAlister now."

Nodding, she moved past him to climb the stairs again to her room. She was accustomed to hard work, but her muscles were protesting her extra exertion, and the burns sent streaks of pain up her calves.

She couldn't resist looking at the bed where Richard lay utterly motionless. The pallor of his washed skin beneath the dark hair tumbling forward across his wide brow was terrifying to see. His high cheekbones outlined bruises beginning to form below the fan of his dark lashes.

"I believe his name is Richard. That was all I found written in this book." Mary whispered, as she always did in sick rooms. "He . . . he is a fine-looking man."

"He's handsome as sin!" Lottie sighed, straightening her nightcap more securely upon her graying gold curls. "What's the likes of him doing in the wilds of Hexham?"

"Perhaps journeying to Edinburgh," Mary offered, moving a step closer to examine the bandages wrapped around Richard's burned hands.

"No matter now. Done all we can until the doctor

arrives. I'll stay with him, Mary." Lottie nodded, new spirit in her voice. "Best for you to wash up and change before Dr. McAlister arrives. I've put a washbowl and towel for you in the sewing room. And best use the salve on yourself, too. Your uncle swears it's a cure for everything from boils to consumption."

Mary took the salve and one of her two serviceable outfits—a plain black bombazine spencer and full skirt—into the tiny sewing room. Her arms and feet throbbed with pain, making her toilette awkward to perform. She couldn't bear to pull on the riding boots she wore every day, so she stepped into her only other shoes, thin silk slippers that were almost like new, although she'd had them for years.

By the time she finished, the salve was already soothing her burns. She hoped it worked as well for Richard.

She moved more easily out into the tiny hall and found her bedroom door closed again. After a morning such as this, a mere closed door was certainly not going to stop her! Lifting her chin, she pushed the door open.

Of the three stunned faces that greeted her entrance, only the doctor's held a faint smile of welcome.

"Miss Masterton, I was just informing your uncle and Miss Barton that we have a serious injury here. Very serious indeed." He emphasized his words with a vigorous shake of his head. "All we can do now is care for his burns and force as much nourishment as possible. If he does not regain consciousness in the next day, I very much doubt that he ever will."

"Poor soul," Lottie breathed, her round face unusually pale.

"Poor soul indeed," the doctor agreed as he closed his traveling bag. "I'll be coming by tomorrow. Let's pray for some change, but I hold out little hope."

"Thank you for coming, Dr. McAlister." Mary flicked him the tiniest of smiles. "We'll do our best for him."

"I'll be showing the doctor out, Mary girl." Uncle Ian said pointedly. "Then I'll be seein' to what's left of the stable and the cause of the fire. Somethin' strange goin' on here. Mighty strange."

"Yes, it is. But we saved the horses. That's the important thing. Please check on them, Uncle Ian. I've fed and watered them, but you'll know better if they're suffering any effects of the fire."

She closed the door quietly behind him and turned to stare at the man whose presence so filled her small, tidy room. Of all the emotions tumbling over one another in her thoughts, one lodged hot and tight in her chest. Guilt forced her to move swiftly to take a stance beside the bed.

"He is grievously injured because he came to our aid." Her whisper came out in a harsh exhalation. "We must do our utmost to help him recover. I shall stay with him while you prepare some thin gruel, Lottie. It will be a good sign if he can take nourishment."

A short time later Lottie returned with a bowl of her special recipe, a gruel to cure all. Determined to care for Richard herself, Mary urged her away to prepare a meal for the rest of them.

Mary very carefully dripped a tiny spoonful of gruel between Richard's dry lips. He swallowed, his strong throat muscles moving, and relief flooded her, with little bubbles of joy popping in her veins. Surely this was an encouraging sign.

She repeated the ritual every two hours all through the day and into the night. At midnight she sent an exhausted Lottie to her room. Uncle Ian had relented enough to admit that there was nothing unseemly about her being alone with such a grievously injured man, particularly one who was unconscious.

The tall clock in the downstairs hall was chiming two as she very slowly unwrapped the bandages from his hands. A heavy gold crest ring slipped off his finger when she reapplied Ian's salve. She studied the chunk of gold resting on her palm, then looked into the face of its wearer.

Lottie had spoken the truth. Even with bruises marking the skin, there was strength and an appealing beauty in the perfect arrangement of flesh knitted to bone in Richard's countenance. She knew little of men, but a great deal of horses. There was a breeding that lent grace to this man, even in his sorry state.

Guilt, which had driven her all through this interminable day, blazed hot and fresh, swelling into her throat. She might never see the eyes now hidden by his hooded lids and dark lashes.

But neither would those who cared about him. Who was he? If he didn't regain consciousness, as the doctor feared, how would they know where to send word?

She quietly lifted the lid of her small rosewood jewel box and placed the ring on top of the seed pearl necklace and earrings she'd had from her mother on her sixteenth birthday. What a sacrifice it must have been for her parents to pay for such a trinket. She lifted out the sapphire ring her mother had been wearing the night she fled with Mary's father to Gretna Green. It wasn't nearly as rich as Richard's signet, but it meant everything to her. It symbolized her parents' love and hopes and dreams. She wouldn't ever let that die; she couldn't!

Nor could she let this man perish because of his kindness to her. Perhaps she could use the ring to help her find his family.

The doctor's dire predictions the next day increased her guilt. Each hour Richard remained unconscious, his chance of recovery diminished. She had to know who he was, how to help him.

Lottie sent her to bed right after supper, insisting she'd done the work of ten that day. Truth to tell, she was exhausted and fell into a dreamless sleep the moment her head rested on the pillow.

But, by one in the morning, judging by the chime of the downstairs clock, she was wide awake, studying the shadows dancing on the ceiling from the dying embers in the small grate. At fifteen minutes after the hour she shook Lottie, who had fallen asleep in the rocker, awake.

She jerked her head back against the curved wood and blinked up in a daze at Mary. "What is it?" she asked in a sleep-slurred whisper.

"Go to your bed, Lottie. I wish to sit with him."

Still slightly groggy, Lottie rose slowly and shook her head. "There's no change. Poor soul." She flicked him one last look before quietly shutting the door.

Mary stared down at him, fear congealing in her chest. He appeared smaller in the bed, as if he were slowly fading away. Suddenly desperate, Mary lifted one bandaged hand, holding it carefully between her palms.

"Richard, my name is Mary." Her harsh whisper fell into the stillness of the tiny room. "I want to thank you for your help. I'm sorry such bravery has cost you so dearly."

She continued talking to him of nothing and everything, as if her words could somehow keep him tethered to life. Late into the night she talked, holding his hand. She told him everything: about her parents and her life, her hopes and her dreams. To her alone here in the dimly lit bedchamber, it seemed the right thing to do.

Toward morning she forced a little more broth through his dry, cracked lips. Exhausted past bearing, she sank into the rocking chair next to the bed.

She awoke to bright sunlight and to Lottie's voice frantically calling her name.

"Mary . . . Mary . . . you must wake up!"

Startled, she quickly glanced toward the bed as her heart raced. The slow, steady rise and fall of the stranger's wide chest beneath the coverlet caused her to gasp and close her eyes in relief. He lived still.

Mary uncurled from the rocker, stretching her aching muscles. "Lottie, whatever is amiss?"

"Sir Robert is downstairs waiting in the parlor," she blurted out, staring at Mary with round, frightened eyes. Everything about Lottie was round, from the fat round curls bobbing behind her ears to the round small feet stuffed into flat-heeled slippers peeking from beneath her hem. Even her mouth pursed into a circle as she gasped. "What should we do? He refuses to leave without seeing you. And your uncle has gone to fetch lumber for the new stable."

Understanding Lottie's fear, Mary patted her arm. "I shall see him. After all, he is our closest neighbor. Please go down and tell him I'll be there directly. Then come back up to stay with Richard. I'll be ready in a trice."

She made a hasty toilette but took the time to put on her best day dress, a blue dimity gown with a blond flounce of lace at the hem. She tugged nervously at the bodice. It had grown a bit tight across her breasts. No matter; she had no choice but to wear it. It was the best she owned, and she needed all her armor against Sir Robert. There was something about him she could not like.

She took her time descending the stairs, her mind racing to find the best course of action for dealing with Sir Robert Lancaster. When she entered the parlor, he rushed toward her with the same eagerness that always made her draw back into a tight ball inside herself.

"Mary, I've been away and just heard the bad news. I came at once to offer my assistance."

She allowed him to clasp her hand for the shortest time dictated by good manners before pulling away. "Thank you, Sir Robert. However, all is well now."

His dark eyes glowed ebony in his swarthy face. "I admire your stubborn determination. I always have. But even you must see this fire spells the end of your dream."

She forced herself to remain in place even as he swayed closer to her, the diamond stickpin in his elegantly arranged cravat blinking into her eyes.

"Mary, I despise the fact that I hold your late

father's vouchers. You have only to accept my offer of marriage, and all his debts of honor will be paid in full. Then together we will go to your grandfather and—"

Flinging back her head, she laughed into his face. "My grandfather won't even acknowledge my existence."

His wide mouth curled in an ingratiating smile. "Of course he doesn't now. Not when you are living with Ian, who is hardly more than a stable hand, and his doxy."

His crude reference to a past Lottie never spoke of froze the knot inside her. Shivering in reaction, she clenched her hands surreptitiously behind her back. He held an enormous sum over her head. She must be civil, or no telling what he'd do to them all.

"Lottie is my friend," she stated quietly, reminding him that he was, after all, a guest in her house. "And as to the other, I've told you time and again that when Lara comes to foal, we'll be able to raise the money you are owed."

"Come, come, Mary!" His hand reached out to flick her cheek. "You've been saying the same for some time now." With his other hand he boldly grabbed one wrist. "I've been patient these many months—" he raised her captured hand to his mouth and let his lips linger over it "—and I find my patience is quite coming to an end."

He pulled her into his arms. Shock and revulsion swept over her, swiftly shifting to hot, trembling rage. With both fists she beat upon his chest.

"Unhand me, sir!" she demanded. When there was no response she pushed harder, an edge of panic cutting sharply along her nerves. "Let me go, or you will answer to my betrothed!" she shouted in desperation.

"What?" His hands dropped away as he stared at her in disbelief.

Carefully she smoothed her gown, struggling for composure. Guilt at the lie and relief that it had served warred within her.

"Yes. I shall be settled very soon, and my father's debts to you paid," she blurted out before she thought better of it. "I am engaged to be married."

"To whom?" he roared, falling back a pace, making it possible for her to breathe more easily.

"His name is Richard." As she warmed to her fantasy, the words tumbled out easily. "Richard Byron," she added, remembering that one of the essays in Richard's book was from Lord Byron's works. "Richard was visiting in the neighborhood, and . . . and we met."

"He plans to pay *all* your debts?" Sir Robert asked with just the veriest edge of sarcasm.

An outrageous plan fell perfectly into place in her mind: if, as the doctor predicted, Richard never regained consciousness, there might be no way to notify his family. So she would use his stallion to stud and the gold ring as collateral for a loan. That way Richard's bravery would not be in vain. If he did recover, as she devotely hoped, well, she'd deal with this lie then.

"Richard would do anything for me!" she declared boldly. In for a penny, in for a pound, Lottie always said. "In fact, he was most grievously injured saving my horses the morning of the fire."

"May I visit him in his sickroom? I wish to offer my felicitations on your upcoming marriage." His smirk was unmistakable. He did not believe her.

"Unfortunately, he is still unconscious from his injury." Even to her own ears it sounded the lamest of excuses.

He had the effrontery to give a bark of laughter. "Mary, really . . ."

"However, if you are very quiet, we can peek in for just a moment."

At last she saw a flicker of doubt shoot through his flat dark eyes. She had allowed him to goad her into this foolishness; now she must see it through. If it rid her once and for all of his distasteful presence, then it would be well worth the lie. This would buy her precious time. Perhaps Richard, or anyone else, need never know about her lie. Lottie she could swear to utter silence.

Lottie's face filled with dismay when they entered the room.

"All is well, Lottie." Mary forced a smile. "Sir Robert merely wishes to pay his respects to my dear Richard."

Ignoring Lottie's gasp of shock, Mary slipped onto the bed to put the final period to Sir Robert's doubts. With gentle fingers she brushed a heavy lock of hair from Richard's brow. Gathering him to her, she leaned over, closed her eyes, and pressed a kiss upon his bruised cheek, near the long, relaxed mouth.

"My darling Richard, I shall never rest until you are restored to me," she murmured with what she hoped sounded like loving devotion. For good measure, she gave one shuddering sigh before lifting her lids.

Shock froze her in place, her arms wrapped protectively around him, her hair enclosing them in privacy. Her supposed intended was awake. She stared into melting chocolate eyes that looked at her in bewilderment.

"It seems I have been, my dear," he whispered, his lips nearly brushing hers.

Chapter 2

*H*is first awareness as he emerged from a black void was the melodious sound of a woman's voice. It surrounded him with vague pleasure as he floated in a nether world, his lids seemingly stuck fast. It was more than he could do to rouse himself to open them.

The touch of gentle fingers across his brow sent shivers of reaction where before there had been numbness. The touch continued along his cheekbone, stroking comfortingly. He could sense her leaning over him, feel her warm breath on his face, and then the faintest touch of her mouth upon his cheek.

"My darling Richard, I shall never rest until you are restored to me."

Her voice held such longing as it caught on a sob. Again he fought the lethargy; who was this angel who called him from the darkness? He felt her hovering over him and, with the greatest act of sheer determination, parted his lids.

The darkness fled as he opened his eyes within a heavy curtain of fragrant auburn hair.

"It seems I have been, my dear." He forced the whisper through his tight, dry throat.

"Richard, you are awake!" she gasped, staring at

him from wide cornflower blue eyes so close that he could see how thickly her lashes grew on the elongated lids.

His mind couldn't quite focus ... visions and thoughts floated just out of his reach.

Richard.

Yes, his name was Richard.

Sharp pain jabbed through his head and down the back of his neck, as he shifted slightly to study her as she abruptly rose from the bed.

Her hair fell in a long, straight auburn mane, framing a pale face dominated by those cornflower eyes slightly tilted up at the corners, giving her a fey look.

She looked like a wild creature of the woods, poised, ready to bolt at the slightest provocation.

"Sir, I'm ever so pleased you're awake!" A small woman spoke from behind the vision.

He turned his head to look at her but couldn't place her. Her round face glowed as she clasped her hands to her ample bosom.

"Mr. Byron, I'm sure we're all delighted at your amazing recovery."

Richard allowed his gaze to slowly move to the swarthy man in impeccable black riding clothes standing at the foot of the bed. His mind might still be as fuzzy as a newborn babe's, but he recognized a sneer in that lazy drawl.

"I am Sir Robert Lancaster. Mary's closest neighbor." His full lips curled in a slight smile. "I want to offer my congratulations on your sudden betrothal to Mary."

Both women gasped! Richard turned too quickly and pain exploded behind his eyes, blurring his vision.

At his grimace of pain, the younger lady—Mary was it?—once again slipped onto the side of his bed.

"Don't tax yourself," she soothed. "We'll leave you to rest now. I shall return with a tray."

"Thank you." He barely breathed the words before she shepherded everyone out, quietly closing the door behind her.

He blinked, his gaze touching the small details of this cozy slope-ceilinged room. The delicate hangings, the carved rosewood jewel box, and a few crystal bottles on the low chest proclaimed this a woman's domain.

Spying a faded mirror over the washstand, he flung back the covers. It took more effort than he had imagined, but somehow he made it the short distance. Supporting himself on flat palms against the oak stand, he stared at his reflection.

Dark hair tumbled around a strong face, the skin marked with bruises beneath hooded eyes. The nose was straight, and the mouth long. He wasn't displeased with the reflection; he was simply looking into the face of a stranger.

He was a stranger! Everything about this place, this room, and these people was unknown to him. Closing his eyes, he tried to capture an elusive shadow shifting back in the utter blankness of his mind.

It eluded him. Opening his eyes again on the countenance of this strange man, he reviewed what he did know.

His name was Richard.

Somehow he knew that was true. It . . . felt correct.

And he was engaged.

He sensed it somehow, back in the emptiness of

31

his mind. Just as he knew he did not love his betrothed.

Damn, why couldn't he remember!

His anger brought such shooting pain through his
skull that he gasped and took a long shuddering
breath. A wave of weakness washed over him. He
had no choice but to stumble back and crawl into
the narrow bed.

The door creaked slowly open a few moments after he'd settled with a deep sigh of relief back upon
the pillows. The fey creature entered, moving with
unconscious grace even though she carried a tray
ladened with a bowl of soup, a generous chunk of
bread with heat still rising from its brown crust,
and a glass of milk.

He eyed the white obnoxious stuff and lifted his
right brow. Instantly he regretted this show of disdain, as a frisson of pain throbbed through his head.

"I would prefer brandy." At least his voice held
a bit more strength than before.

Suddenly her thin face was transformed by a
smile that brought dancing lights to the cornflower
eyes, and a deep dimple appeared beside the sweetly
curved cherry lips.

"I'm quite sure you would," she laughed, a mu-
sical sound that was oddly soothing to his aching
head. "However, until the doctor arrives, I fear I
cannot offer you spirits."

She set the tray on the stand beside the bed and
unfolded the napkin to lay beneath his chin. "Uncle Ian has gone for him."

"Mary, how long have we been engaged?" His
blunt question banished her enchanting smile, and
he saw blood flow brightly beneath the fine trans-

lucent skin of her face. How could he *not* love such an enchanting creature?

"Richard, I must tell . . ."

Whatever she was about to say was lost as the door creaked open.

"Mary my girl, met the doctor at the front gate. Comin' to check on our patient."

Pain shot up his neck as he pushed himself higher on the pillows.

"Jeffries!" The name burst out of him on a wave of acute relief. At last, someone he knew!

His elation lasted only a moment, receding as quickly as it had come, for the wiry man with the riotous red hair and beard shook his head.

"No, lad, I'm Ian Masterton, Mary's uncle."

He closed his eyes against the disappointment, racking his foggy brain for answers. He knew someone named Jeffries. A man who greatly resembled Mary's uncle.

A sense of great fondness lapped at the edges of his empty mind. Then sorrow pierced the blackness. Jeffries was dead. He didn't know how or when; he just knew it was true.

"Well, sir, let us see how you are doing."

The doctor's voice brought him back to this new world populated by a man who tugged at his lost memories and a fiancée who looked frightened to death of him. She cast him one final glance from troubled eyes before she fled the room.

The doctor, also unknown to him, smiled. "Now, sir, tell me how you are feeling."

He met Ian Masterton's steady eyes before allowing his gaze to rest on the far wall. "It seems whatever accident befell me robbed me of my memory." His lazy drawl shocked him. The next moment he smiled, settling deeper into the pillows; these slightly sarcastic tones rang true. "I have no recognition of this place nor any idea who I am."

"Mary, what are you about? That poor soul looked as innocent as a babe when he heard of your engagement. I fair fainted on the spot! Why would you tell Sir Robert such an outrageous story?"

Lottie's frantic questions beset Mary at every turn as she paced outside the bedroom door. Caught in a web of her own making! But she needn't fear Lottie. Lottie would understand, and so would the stranger when she explained all to him.

"Sir Robert was being . . ." Just remembering his touch begat a shudder deep inside her. ". . . obnoxious. And . . . and it just came out." She shook her head in wonder at her foolishness. "I thought if Richard did not regain consciousness I would use his stallion to stud and his ring as collateral while we searched for his family. And if he did awaken, I would confess all and throw myself on his mercy."

Lottie gazed at her in open-mouthed awe. It brought home her determination to tell the stranger all, and she rushed on, "I tried to tell him the truth earlier, but I was interrupted."

"Thank the good God you were interrupted if you intend to tell my patient anything that will upset him!" The doctor's stern voice brought Mary to an utter standstill. The look on his face as he shut her bedroom door sent hot dread swelling in her chest.

"What is it? He isn't worse!"

"No, no, Mary my girl," Ian soothed, placing a bracing hand on her shoulder. "Listen to what Dr. McAlister be tellin' us."

The doctor favored them all with a hard stare.

"We have a serious problem here. Very serious indeed!" He emphasized his words with a vigorous shake of his head. "Because of his injury, Mr. Byron is suffering from memory loss. All he recalls is the name Richard; a friend, Jeffries, who greatly resembled Ian; and his engagement to Mary."

"What!" Mary's heart nearly stopped from the shock. Suddenly the air thinned around her and she gasped, "But we are not—"

Holding up his palm, the doctor stopped her rush of words. "I don't ken what's going on here, young lady. I only know what is best for my patient. He must have no shocks. None whatsoever!" he stressed, holding Mary's stunned gaze. "Whatever the truth of his past, he must be allowed to remember it naturally. If not, I fear it might bring on a brain fever. Indeed, then we *would* lose him forever."

He softened his words with the slightest of smiles. "Now give him whatever he wishes. I heard him muttering something about brandy. A wee bit wouldn't hurt."

"I'll fetch it at once!" Lottie picked up the hem of her skirt to rush down the narrow steps.

"I'll show myself out," Dr. McAlister chuckled, following her down. "You won't need me again, unless you go against my orders."

Ian wasted no time, staring at Mary from beneath bushy sandy brows. "Mary girl, best be tellin' me the truth of things."

She told him as quickly as she could, with the guilt burning in her stomach spreading upward to fill her chest, and then her throat, until she ended, sobbing softly.

"Mary girl, you will leave Sir Robert to me!"

Ian's wiry body grew rigid as he spread his legs in a wide stance of defiance. "Your father's debts are as much my responsibility as yours. He was tryin' to fulfill the dream we'd had since we were lads."

"And his dream for me." She clasped her uncle's outstretched hands. "He wished to leave me something of substance to make up for what he believed I was missing. I only wish to make sure we don't lose everything he worked so hard to achieve."

"You'll see, Mary my girl. We'll find a way to pay off Sir Robert. Even with the setback of the stable fire."

Warmed by the strength of his grip and his words, she nodded. "First we must pay our debt to Richard. I swear I shall help him regain his memory so I can confess my falsehood. He will understand, won't he, Uncle Ian? A man that good, who would stop to help strangers with a fire . . ." The words died away as Lottie appeared clutching a crystal decanter of brandy in one hand and a glass in the other.

Mary whisked them from her hand. "I wish to take it to him." Guilt and new purpose driving her, she plastered a wide smile on her face and opened the door.

Richard had elbowed himself higher on the pillows so that Ian's white nightshirt stretched tightly across his chest, outlining rippling muscles. She could hardly keep from staring at him. He ran long fingers through his hair, sending the heavy waves away from his brow, as he watched her with hooded eyes. Obviously he believed her lie, for he was so . . . natural with her. But what she was experiencing was hardly natural.

"Your new medicine from the doctor, sir." She

bobbed down in a curtsy, handing him the glass, trying to diffuse her tension. Still watching her carefully, he took it and tilted the entire contents down his throat.

His long mouth curled at the corners in a smile. "Another memory returned. I much prefer brandy to milk."

She answered his lazy smile with one of her own as she slipped down into the curved chair beside the bed, suddenly more at ease.

"I know you have lost much of your memory. I want to help you regain it."

Even in the few minutes she had been away from him, pacing the hall, his expressive hooded eyes had grown sharper. He rested that bright gaze steadily on her face.

"Your uncle told me I'm at your home in Hexham. Tell me about the accident. How long have I been here? When did we become betrothed?"

The doctor's warning rang in her ears as she searched for the right words. "I'm not supposed to tease you with memories. The doctor said they must come naturally." She evaded his questions. "Would you like to hear about the accident? You were so brave that morning!" Her soft voice gained strength as she realized that in this she could be utterly truthful. "The stable was an inferno, but you were fearless. We would have been unable to save all the horses without your help. You were bringing out the last two colts when the falling beam struck you."

A furrow worried his smooth brow. "I feel I'm fond of horses. Did they escape unharmed?"

"Oh, yes, thanks to you! Do you remember your

stallion?" she asked eagerly. "He is the most mar-
velous Arabian I've ever seen."

The hooded eyes became mere slits as he considered. "Damn it! Nothing!"

When he lifted his lids she saw the frustration,
just as she'd heard it in his voice. Terrified by the
white strained line around his long mouth, she desperately searched for a way to reassure him.

"Don't tax yourself. The memories shall return
in time."

Suddenly inspired, she went quickly to her jewel
box and returned to the bed with the heavy crested
ring on her palm.

"This is your ring. Does it bring back any memories? Anything at all?"

He took the ring carefully, running his fingertips
over the raised crest and feeling the weight of the
gold. "It appears to be a fine ring. Too rich for me."
He shot her a rueful look. "But it means nothing.
Keep it. It would only be a bother while I work."

Reaching out he lifted one of her hands, placed
the ring on the palm, and curled her fingers over
it. "Tomorrow I'll be up. There is much to do if the
stable is to be rebuilt."

The idea that he would help them further shocked
her. "You shall do no such thing! You must rest
and regain your strength."

"I'll regain my strength faster once I'm on my
feet." He flexed his broad shoulders restlessly, pulling the shirt wide so that she spied a large expanse
of smooth, muscled chest. "As your future husband
it's my duty to help you. After all, isn't this to be
our home once we're wed?"

Unable to utter one more lie, Mary simply nodded, appalled at the path one moment of panic was forcing her down.

"It's late. Rest now. I shall see you in the morning."

She fairly bolted from the room, but at the door glanced back to find him watching her with a deep scowl. He didn't remember her either! Well of course not, why would he? But why did he accept their engagement so readily? Even saying it was one of the few things he did remember? Unless he was truly engaged. That thought pulled her up short. Richard must be engaged to someone. Someone who would be wondering about him, missing him. Opening her clenched fist, she stared down at the gold ring.

She knew what she must do.

"Whatever shall I do?" Lady Arabella Hampton wailed as only she could, and very prettily too, as she paced the Aubusson carpet of the Avalon morning room with such determined steps that the lilac ruffle of her walking gown flipped up, revealing matching kid half boots. "The Duchess of Cumberland's Grand Ball is tomorrow and Richard hasn't returned! That beast! The entire ton heard me threaten to cry off. I have been reliably informed that bets are on at White's I shall do so before midnight! What can I do?"

This last wail was so strident that Wilkens peeped in from the hall. Her Grace, the Duchess of Avalon, was forced to abandon her worries about her restless son Richard and face the problem at hand: Lady Arabella Hampton, his betrothed.

The duchess, a noted bluestocking, rarely, if ever, gave advice. She merely allowed her offspring to follow the path of their true leanings. "Bella, dear, tell me what *you* wish to do."

"I wish to go to the Duchess of Cumberland's Grand Ball!"

Arabella's flushed face filled her with deep sadness. This choice of Richard's was so foreign to the path his intellect usually led him down. Even though their families had been friends for generations and once, long ago, a match had been spoken of, Richard had not been forced to follow this course. Did he believe he could take this unformed clay and mold it into a vessel of his choice?

She only wished for Richard what she'd had with his father; what her younger son, Matthew, had with his sweet Serena; and what her impetuous daughter, Cecily, had with her dashing Kendall.

Was there a woman anywhere who could truly capture his elusive regard? The duchess knew that if such a woman existed, she would needs fight through the many layers that made up her complex son, but the prize, if won, would be indeed wonderful.

The petulant girl before her, who had slipped into the pout that made her the darling of the ton, was not the woman for her son. She knew it as surely as she knew that Bella deserved to find her own perfect match.

Realizing that she had been rude by her pensive silence, the duchess smiled. "Bella, I fully appreciate your dilemma. You could of course ask one of your court of admirers to take you in Richard's place. But, alas, that would only set the tongues wagging anew. No doubt there would be betting at White's that you had chosen another."

"So you see, I am undone!" the young girl sobbed in earnest, her eyes filling with angry tears.

The duchess rose to offer comfort just as the doors opened soundlessly.

"Lord Frederick Charlesworth to see you, Your Grace," Wilkens announced in the deep voice that added importance to every one of his pronouncements.

"How fortuitous," the duchess sighed, relaxing back onto the green velvet settee. "You will attend the ball with Lord Charlesworth. He's my sweet Serena's cousin. Practically a member of the Avalon family. It would be most natural for Charlesworth to be Avalon's envoy in his absence."

She saw the idea click into place in Arabella's eyes even before Frederick strolled into the room.

The change in his appearance still amazed the duchess even after nearly eighteen months. He had been in Brussels with his doting mama during the war, a dandy of such alarming proportions he'd been a laughingstock. Richard had reported that Frederick had escorted Serena to the battlefield to find her husband Matthew when no one else would, and he'd returned a changed man.

She'd been as shocked as the rest of the ton when Richard, whose every protegé became the darling of society, chose to bring Frederick into fashion. It just showed another side of her older son, that he had taken Charlesworth under his wing, without mockery or his usual sarcastic boredom, and had helped him slowly emerge into the man who stood before her: a kind-hearted young man, with soft brown hair brushed in a style all his own that framed a face dominated by huge owl eyes. But, complemented by the confident smile that he now

41

wore easily, the enormous features appeared poetically appealing.

"Charlesworth, we were just speaking of you."

Bending over her hand, he blinked at her words, somewhat taken aback.

"Lady Arabella and I are hoping you will do us a great service."

"For two such lovely ladies, anything!" he declared with easy gallantry.

"We wish you to be Richard's envoy and escort Lady Arabella to the Duchess of Cumberland's Grand Ball tomorrow."

For just an instant the owl eyes stretched alarmedly, but a moment later they settled, with appealing crinkles at the corners. "With great pleasure." He made a very pretty bow in Bella's direction.

"Good," Arabella retorted with another of her pouts. "I shall look forward to it, sir." With a toss of her head she swept out of the room.

The duchess met Charlesworth's eyes, and they both smiled in agreement.

"Old Long's really in for it when he returns," Frederick laughed, using Richard's childhood nickname. "Have you heard from him, Your Grace? London's a dull place without him."

The niggling worry returned. It was unlike Richard to be so careless. Usually he kept her well-informed of his whereabouts or, at least, one of his servants could always locate him. But not even Crowley, who she knew was waiting impatiently in Edinburgh, knew of Richard's whereabouts.

It was as if her son had simply disappeared.

Chapter 3

From the sewing room window Mary watched the dawn slide over her land, as it slowly turned the spring green grass emerald, banishing the shadows from the makeshift lean-to for the horses, before it finally burst into the yard.

The dull thud of the back door closing behind her uncle roused her fully. There was much to be done this beautiful day.

In three days, Ian and two men he'd hired from the village already had the main supports up and the roof nearly complete on the new stable. At least now they could bed the horses down under shelter to protect them from any sudden rains.

So her uncle could have no excuse for rejecting the plan she'd agonized over at night, tossing and twisting on her narrow cot in the cozy sewing room. Richard was comfortably ensconced in her bedchamber, and there he would remain until this coil that her foolishness had entangled them in was unwound and all made right. She now knew how that task could be accomplished quickly.

She flew through her toilette, hastily putting on one of her serviceable bombazine dresses. She wound a black ribbon around her heavy hair at the nape to keep it tidy.

Ignoring breakfast, she made her way to where Uncle Ian stood in the stable yard issuing orders to the men up on the roof.

"Uncle Ian, I must speak with you."

He turned, eyes crinkled by the sun, to smile at her. "Why, Mary my girl, you're up and about early. Come to see how the new stable be farin'."

"I can see it's going wonderfully well. So well that by tomorrow you should be able to leave for London."

"Now why would I be goin' to London?" he asked gruffly, folding powerful arms across his chest.

"To take Richard's ring to my grandfather's solicitor. Perhaps he can trace the crest and locate Richard's family." She held his steady gaze, and for good measure tilted her chin higher. "Surely you can see it is the best way to help him."

"Come away now." He led her away from the workers toward the horses, where they could be private. "Aye, I can see you're fair eaten up with guilt about your lie. And I can see that finding Richard's family would be just the thing."

His steely stare dissolved as his eyes softened and his mouth curled up in the kind smile that she'd come to love. There was a remarkable resemblance to her father in his suddenly sweet face, although John Masterton's hair had been auburn like hers, not the fiery red of Ian's. Memories of her dear father brought a hot lump into her throat. Swallowing the pain, she reached out, tightly clasping her uncle's rough, callused hands.

"Please do this. I know it will be for the best."

Ian took her hands in a strong grip and shook his head. "I can't be leavin' the stable half-done. Be-

44

sides, after the fire and Sir Robert's visit I'm not for leavin' you unprotected."

"She won't be unprotected, Ian. I'm here." The sound of Richard's voice, strong and determined, came from behind her.

She twisted around. The first time she'd seen Richard he'd been a black silhouette wavering through thick gray smoke. Now the sun's brightness hid his face from her, while it outlined his broad shoulders and his long lean form as he stood with his legs braced apart.

She blinked, shading her eyes as he strolled over, as if he'd just arisen from a restful sleep instead of crawling out of a sickbed. A sickbed he was in because he'd helped her! She'd managed to keep him there, over his protests, for these few days. Now here he was, fully dressed, and she didn't know quite what to expect.

"Richard, you shouldn't be up. It's too soon!"

He slid her a look that brought a flush all the way to her fingertips. "As you can see, I'm fine. Except for a blasted headache, which comes and goes. No doubt the fresh air will help."

Dismissing her concerns with one glance from those hooded eyes, he turned to her uncle. "If you must be away on business, I can handle whatever arises here."

Mary didn't miss the challenge in Richard's drawl.

Squinting, Ian gave him a measuring look. "Aye, I can see you would. Can you recall ever building a stable, lad?"

Richard shrugged carelessly and led Ian toward the work site, pointing out several improvements that could be made. She watched her uncle's reactions, surprised by her own readiness to trust this stranger. Then he turned and glanced at her, catching her curious gaze.

"No, I don't remember ever building a stable. But I feel I'm a quick learner," he drawled slowly, his words for Ian, but his eyes slowly searching her face.

With an effort that left her breathless, she met the curious intensity burning in his stare and smiled. "Then Uncle Ian can rest easy leaving you in charge."

"Aye, I reckon I'm for London on the morrow."

She slipped away as Richard and Ian turned back to work. She found Lottie in the kitchen. Taking a chunk of her bread, Mary toasted it carefully on the end of a long fork, squatting in front of the fireplace as she'd done as a child.

When she told Lottie about Ian's trip the woman bustled around the room beaming. "You're such a good girl. You be doing what's right."

The kind words did little to appease the load of guilt she carried. She was painfully aware that "good girls" did not tell outrageous lies about being engaged to handsome men of obvious wealth, no matter the provocation. But she was doing all she could to make up for it.

She spent the morning helping Lottie, who decided that every window needed to be cleaned inside and out. It wasn't hard work, but she experienced a real sense of accomplishment, and it wasn't so hard to push the guilty burden to the back of her mind.

At noon, Ian and Richard came in for a hasty luncheon of fowl accompanied by two side dishes and a custard with berries. She was pleased to see

Richard's robust appetite. Obviously being up and about was good for him. And yet, the intensity of his dark brown eyes made an odd nervousness tingle along her skin. Her fingers trembled ever so slightly as she lifted a teacup to her lips.

"Mary, are you tired? I put fresh linens on the cot in the sewing room. Why don't you rest after luncheon," Lottie urged, her round face narrowing in concern.

"I'm fine, really." She loved Lottie dearly, but sometimes it was difficult to be surrounded by people who knew one so well and were so . . . noticing.

"There is much to do before Uncle Ian leaves for London."

"Why are you sleeping in the sewing room?"

Richard's husky voice distracted her. The words were barely spoken when she saw knowledge flash into his eyes. "Lottie, are there also fresh linens in the room where I'm staying?" His lazy drawl didn't reveal what he was thinking, and his eyes were hooded by those heavy lids.

Lottie responded with a warm chuckle. "My, yes. All fresh and rinsed in heather. You should rest, too, Richard."

Pushing to his feet, he shook his head. "No. As Mary said, there is much to do." He waited for Ian to rise from the table. The two men, in perfect charity with one another, left, discussing the work projected for the morrow.

Lottie turned to her with a mock shiver. She wrapped her plump arms across her breasts and smiled so broadly her rosy cheeks looked like ripe apples. "Besides being handsome as sin, he's a deep one is our Richard."

Mary wouldn't agree. If she acknowledged his attractive qualities out loud, she would be lost. He was a veritable wonder—helping rebuild the stable, grooming the horses, being so easy with Lottie and Uncle Ian, and all the while sending her those special glances that tickled along her nerve endings and made her increasingly uneasy.

It was almost as if he belonged here. As if he were truly her betrothed. She couldn't allow herself to think along those lines, to wish for something that could never be.

Later in the afternoon she carried a basket of tea out into the yard, determined to tell him the truth. He appeared so strong and healthy. Surely the doctor's fears were unfounded; such a man as Richard would be able to withstand the truth.

She found him asleep, sitting in the tall grass against the large oak behind the cottage. His strong face was dissolved into soft lines of vulnerability, much as it had been during the fearful time she'd nursed him. Gone was the sardonic veneer that slipped naturally over him when he was fully awake and aware.

"He's a right one," Ian suddenly whispered beside her. "Quality like you, Mary my girl, or my name's not Ian Masterton."

Mary, too tired to argue this old discussion, let the comment slide by and handed her uncle the basket of tea things. "He has been nothing but helpful to us, at the cost of his own health. And I repay him with a lie." Unconsciously she lifted her chin, a habit whenever she had to face difficulties. "Has he remembered anything more about his past?"

"Only that he knows horseflesh. Better than any man I know." The fiery mustache and short beard separated in a wide grin. "Wild to get back on that stallion of his. I'll be takin' him into the village. We'll have a pint and a bit of supper at the White Feathers. Richard should be meetin' the lads 'round here if I'm to be away, just in case there's trouble. Are you tellin' him why I'm for London?"

She stared down at Richard, the doctor's words beating in her mind. He didn't look strong now; he appeared younger and infinitely more vulnerable. She couldn't jeopardize him further. "No. It might only raise false hope. Let us see what transpires in London. Mayhap it will be something that helps him regain his memory."

She went back to the house without waking him. She would just have to trust that the ring would bring them some news.

By the time Richard and her uncle rode slowly toward the village, she was convinced she was doing the right thing. He looked so natural atop his stallion. He rode like he was one with the horse.

An ache in her chest rose up to her throat. With one finger she absently stroked her neck and drew in a long sweet breath. He may have lost his memory, but not his instinct with horses. Who was he? What was such a man doing in this wild border county? How had he arrived at the moment when they so desperately needed help?

That memory led naturally to a contemplation of all her problems, chiefly the weight of her father's enormous debt to Sir Robert. It just didn't seem believable! How had her dear father ever incurred so much debt? And how could she ever pay it back and still make his dream of a horse farm profitable? She wouldn't be able to put Sir Robert off much longer.

Goose bumps raised the hair on her arms as a chill pierced her body to its very center. Acquiescing to Sir Robert and his suggestion that her debt would be paid the day they wed was unthinkable. It was equally impossible to appeal to her grandfather, a man she'd never met, and knew only from the miniature her mother had tucked away in a trunk with all the other trappings of her former life. From all the stories her mother had told, she knew that her grandfather was a hard and unforgiving man.

But perhaps his solicitor would aid her search for Richard's identity. That task had to be her first concern. Only when it was completed could she concentrate on how to save the land her father had struggled so hard to keep.

Following their light supper, she helped Lottie ready Ian's bags for the journey to London before she sent her off to bed. After careful consideration and several tries, she was finally happy with the letter of explanation to the solicitor who quarterly sent the meager stipend that was her portion from her grandmother's dowry. She turned Richard's ring over and over in her hand, studying the unfamiliar crest, feeling its weight settle around her heart. If only she could forget about it and go through with the charade—how pleasant it would be if she could truly deposit all her cares on Richard's broad and capable shoulders. It would be delightful to continue under his protection as her betrothed. But she couldn't allow this fantasy to continue. She really could count on no one but herself to set things to rights.

Exhausted, she rose from the chair in the sewing room and slipped into her own chamber to gather up a fresh nightshift from her cupboard before Richard returned.

She first felt his presence by a piercing hot awareness of being watched. She trembled ever so slightly as she turned to face the door. He stood framed in the narrow rectangle. The heavy waves of his hair were black with moisture. Droplets of water glistened on his chest where the lawn shirt separated, and the fine fabric molded to his damp skin.

"I see Uncle Ian showed you the pond." Her voice sounded so husky that she swallowed, trying to ease her suddenly dry throat.

"Yes. Have we ever swum together there by moonlight, Mary?"

His question was so intimate that she was stunned into silence. Even when he moved so close that the fresh scent of his clean skin enveloped her, she didn't stir. Nor did she withdraw into the tight cold ball inside that formed everytime Sir Robert came near her.

He lifted his hand and stroked her cheek with one gentle finger. Suddenly her limbs seemed to be liquid and, for one wild moment, she wondered what held her erect.

"I'm sorry I don't remember you more clearly, Mary. I'm sorry I've kept you from your room." His hushed voice flowed around her, weaving a spell that shook her to her very core.

"I'm returning it to you tonight." His hooded eyes slid slowly down her body, and in their depths shadows shifted. "Until we share it together."

In all her nineteen years, there had been nothing that taught her how to behave when faced with a man who falsely believed they were soon to be wed, and who might fall into a fatal illness if he learned the truth. Surely there was some protection; he was a gentleman and, poor or not, she knew she was a gentlewoman. She should be discreet. She should withdraw.

Instead, she closed her eyes. She felt his breath on her cheek. Then his mouth touched hers gently; her lips parted in a silent gasp of surprise.

Instantly his mouth claimed hers, his tongue stroking the soft openness as his fingers cupped her hot cheeks. She was unable to move, unable to stop the new sensations rushing to all parts of her body. He dragged his lips across hers again, and again, until the contours of her mouth altered, swelling and molding to the supple shape of his. This pulsing sweetness was a new world for Mary, black, shot with flashes of gold and red, bursting through her blood like sparks of fire.

She whimpered deep in her throat, and his sweet mouth slid across her cheek to the shell of her ear, where it lingered. His breath against that sensitive skin made her sway under the powerful new feelings he stirred to life.

It was too much, even for someone of Mary's considerable spirit. Lifting trembling hands, she laid them against his warm chest, pushed gently, and opened her eyes.

The candlelight softened his face with aching vulnerability as he captured her shaking fingers, stilling their futile fluttering.

"It's all right, Mary," he said softly, opening one hand to press his lips against her palm. He held her dazed eyes with a burning sherry-washed glow. "Rest well, my dear."

He turned and walked from the room. Her nightshift lay in a heap at her feet, unnoticed. Her body began to shake in reaction, her fingers lifting in wonder to her mouth. Richard! What had she done with that momentary lapse, that simple lie?

She was out of her depth, drawn there by her own foolishness and her first budding knowledge of physical desire. Frightened by its powerful pull, she rocked back and forth, her thoughts focused on only one thing. More than ever before, she realized how desperately important it was for Richard's memory to return.

From the sewing room window Richard watched Mary and Lottie bid Ian farewell. Not wishing to intrude, he stayed upstairs, content to study Mary at leisure: her long auburn hair falling down her straight back to her tiny waist. Even from this distance he could see her wide fawn eyes fill with tears and her full, red, luscious lips tremble slightly.

Why didn't he love her? She was beautiful. She was good. She was sensitive. She was a tireless worker and devoted to her family. She appeared to be all a woman should be. So why didn't he love her?

He waged a constant battle against the wall in his mind, but there were few answers. And the little bits and pieces he chipped away were even more confusing. That was why he'd kissed her, he told himself. To try to understand.

Was she a cold, passionless woman? Was that why theirs was to be a marriage of convenience? Or was he simply untouched by her unconventional beauty? Instinctively he knew that she was unlike any other woman in his life. He was certain that must be the answer to the puzzle.

Kissing her had unleashed within him the eroticism of an experienced lover. Mary had met that

53

with an edge of passion that stirred him, even now, as he remembered. He might not love her, but he now knew that he desired her. Successful marriages had been built on less.

Mary watched until Ian was out of sight, then turned to the field and gave a sharp whistle. Lara trotted up and waited patiently while Mary fitted her with a new bridle and saddle. Her usual tack had been lost in the fire, and Richard had been surprised at the fuss Ian had made at the cost of new. Over drinks at the tavern he'd gotten a little more information about the farm, but enough could be read between the lines to understand that Mary was shouldering a large debt since her parent's death.

She rode off with the same unconscious grace with which she did everything. Suddenly eager to learn more about her, about them, Richard turned from the window. If he hurried, he could follow her.

Just as he sprang onto his horse, Lottie came bustling through the garden gate.

"I wish to catch up with Mary. Where does she usually ride, Lottie?"

She pushed one fat gold curl off her forehead with a finger that left a flour streak, and nodded. "I know just the spot. Along the water and round about the pond."

He knew the way from last night. The stream wound like a loose ribbon through the meadow from beyond the town to a nearby river. At one point near the cottage it widened, and a natural formation of rock created a pool overhung by willows and perfumed by lily of the valley clinging to its banks.

The clear water with the moon reflected on its smooth surface had been too much to resist last night. The shock of the cold as he dived in had washed the last lingering lethargy from his limbs, but it had done nothing to clear the cobwebs of his mind. He must resign himself to the reality of his helplessness. It seemed almost as if his life had begun when he opened his eyes within the fragrant curtain of Mary's hair.

The sudden thought that perhaps he would come upon Mary swimming brought a hot clutching tightness low in his gut.

Driven on by that image, he crested the low hill, then reined sharply at the tableau that greeted him. On the bank Mary and Sir Robert sat talking, so close that their horses nuzzled one another familiarly.

Was this why he couldn't understand his mixed reactions to her, because he knew she had another lover?

Something unpleasant boiled in his blood. He urged his horse forward. Then Sir Robert reached out, covering Mary's hand with his own. Richard reined to a halt in front of them, and they both glanced up.

With a start of shock, Sir Robert pulled back. But the flash of relief on Mary's face answered at least part of the riddle. This was no lover. She despised and feared this man. That he would deal with later.

"Mr. Byron, rumor has it you have yet to regain your memory, but how delightful to see you out and about so soon after your accident." Sir Robert spoke quickly, as if to cover some unpleasantness.

Richard lifted one brow slightly. "I've missed my usual ride with *my* beautiful fiancée," he said, enunciating each word with care.

He could tell he'd made his point by the slight widening of Sir Robert's eyes. Mary's fingers tightened on her reins. Before she could bolt, he urged his horse between them. With deliberate slowness he reached out, running his fingers from Mary's shoulder lightly down her arm, until his hand covered hers as Sir Robert's had briefly done.

"Mary and I have much to catch up on," he drawled, holding her wide frightened gaze.

"I can see I'm definitely *de trop* here!" Sir Robert backed away, but instead of capitulating completely, as Richard expected, he continued in a challenging tone. "Mary, I'll stop by later so we can finish our discussion."

Richard could feel Mary's fingers tremble beneath his hand. Without a backward glance he moved away at a brisk trot, taking Mary's reins in his hands, making her follow. At the top of the hill, he stopped and returned them to her.

"I don't remember Sir Robert Lancaster. Enlighten me," he teased deliberately. "Why don't we like him?"

The sunlight graced her, coloring the creamy skin of her high cheekbones and turning the uptilted fey eyes a dazzling blue.

"It's not that we don't like Sir Robert," she explained slowly, gazing up at him with an innocent unblinking stare. "There are business dealings he had with my late father, which are unfortunately still not resolved."

"How can I help?"

The simple question brought Mary's lashes sweeping down, concealing her eyes. A tightness hardened her soft mouth and flowed through her entire body. Richard could feel her tension and her withdrawal. Whatever was between her and Sir

Robert Lancaster, he'd get to the bottom of it, and soon!

"It . . . it isn't your problem, Richard." Her words were spoken so softly that he was forced to lean closer to catch them.

"My dear, if we are to be wed, all your problems are mine to solve."

"Of course," she gasped, flinging up her head, but still not able to meet his searching gaze. "We must be getting back. Lottie will have your breakfast ready." She urged her horse away, flinging the words over her shoulder.

He let her go, pausing to stare back to where Sir Robert Lancaster remained at the bank. There was a pattern forming in his new world: Mary's unease with him, and the underlying shadow of fear that she couldn't quite hide around Sir Robert. How did this man fit into the puzzle that was now Richard's life?

Sir Robert watched them go, black anger raging beneath the bland exterior he had long ago learned to project.

How dare that fool Richard Byron upset his carefully laid plans! He had had Mary exactly where he wished. He had done exactly what the old Baron paid him handsomely to do. But now that old tyrant was in for an unpleasant surprise.

His laughter echoed across the stream, the sound rustling around him as he urged his horse home to Landsdown.

He had his own plans for Miss Mary Masterton. And he wasn't about to let any upstart overset them. The obvious, and increasingly necessary, plum of Mary's unlikely connection to wealth was but one of her attractions. Beneath her cool exterior he could see hidden sexuality, evidenced in the unconscious grace of her movements and her full pouty mouth. He would vastly enjoy whatever of her inheritance he could wheedle or blackmail from her grandfather, but what would bring him even greater pleasure would be possessing her. Then he would make her pay for the revulsion that she couldn't hide whenever he was near her.

Nothing would stop him. Certainly not a man who couldn't even recall his own name!

Chapter 4

"It's Sir Robert!" Lottie hissed, letting the cream lace curtain drop into place. She turned from the parlor window, her eyes round and her plump hands twisting together in agitation. "Why does he always pop in when we're alone? Richard's gone off to the village to fetch the last of the lumber needed for the stable."

That she must once again deal with Sir Robert Lancaster was a mere annoyance. Her mind was totally preoccupied with thoughts of Richard. The worst had happened! She was coming to rely on him as if he truly were her fiancée. He worked tirelessly alongside the men rebuilding the stable. He exercised the horses with her, his gentle touch with the creatures in accord with her own theories on how they should be trained. Often she caught him watching her from beneath those mesmerizing hooded eyelids. All this week Richard had filled her every waking hour and haunted her nights.

An odd nervousness was building between them, especially since those shocking moments up in her room. Although he'd not touched her in any way since that night, she knew instinctively that he would again. But when? And terrifying her to her very core was her uncertainty of how she would re-act when that moment finally arrived.

"Mary?" Lottie questioned anxiously, her face telling her fears.

"Never worry, Lottie. I shall handle Sir Robert." Mary prided herself on just the right note of confidence in her words.

Their effect on Lottie was just as she'd hoped. Her round chin firmed and jutted in the air as she flung the front door wide and gave Sir Robert the briefest of nods.

He spared her hardly a glance, striding purposefully into the parlor. As always, his impeccable black riding clothes and shining hessians contrasted sharply with the shabby, but lovingly cared-for, possessions in the cozy blue and cream parlor.

Uppermost in Mary's mind was the lie she was living. She was depending on her uncle's quest in London so that all could be resolved. These petty problems with Sir Robert paled in comparison. She'd put him off successfully since her father's death. Surely she could continue to do so a while longer.

He crossed the room to reach her, forcefully lifting her resistant hand to his mouth.

Immediately the icy ball rolled through her middle, sending a shiver of revulsion up her arm. There was something new in Sir Robert's eyes, a cruel insistence that frightened her. She had all she could do to endure the brush of his lips against her skin and maintain a fixed smile of welcome.

"Mary, you're looking particularly lovely today."

His words rang as false as his smile, which did not reach into his cold gray eyes.

"Thank you, sir. Won't you sit down." She indicated the faded striped wing chair beside the worn blue velvet settee where she sat.

Much to her discomfort, he chose to sprawl beside her, his leg brushing her skirt. She stiffened, sitting bolt upright as he cavalierly slid his arm along the back of the settee, as if he might touch her hair. He threw a disdainful glance at the tea service on the low table before her.

"I could do with something a bit stronger!" He threw the rude words into the room, eyeing Lottie as a boorish employer might a recalcitrant servant.

"Would you care for brandy, Sir Robert?" Mary inquired coolly, grateful to have an excuse to rise to her feet.

He reached out to lock one hand about her wrist; she froze in rigid indignation, hardly knowing what to do. He was getting bolder with each meeting. If only Richard were present, or Uncle Ian, she amended hastily.

"We need to talk, Mary. About your father's debts."

Why had she never noticed before how cruel he appeared when his mouth curled in this cross between a sneer and a smile?

"I'll fetch Sir Robert's brandy," Lottie gasped with round-eyed fear. "I shall be but a moment."

Mary extricated her hand and sat as far from him as possible, busying herself with her own dish of tea.

"You realize, Mary, all your problems could be so easily solved. You can't have been blind these months to my feelings for you."

The oily, coaxing tones were almost amusing. First he intimidated her, now he was pretending an attachment. What could the man want? No debt was worth being leg-shackled to a person she despised.

"Marry me and set all to rights," he urged in a hoarse voice.

She put her tea down and clasped her fingers together in her lap to cover their betraying tremble.

"Sir, you forget, I am promised to another!"

Her retort merely made him smile and sway closer. "He doesn't even remember you. God's blood! I was only gone a fortnight! Your affections can't have been engaged so quickly."

The touch of his fingers brushing her cheek brought such a lurch of revulsion that she feared she would become ill.

"Sir Robert—"

He stopped her croak. "Mary, you know we belong together! Just think of your father's dream. If we marry, your lands will merge with mine. This Richard can't offer you that! But I can give you the horse farm your father wished for!"

As if he could see into her heart and feel that uneven catch in her breath at mention of her father, he pressed his slight advantage. Before she quite realized what was happening, he held her shoulders cupped in his wide palms.

"Cry off from this ridiculous entanglement. It's false and you know it!"

She sensed the instant her guilty expression gave her away by his sudden painful grip and the stunned widening of his cold gray eyes.

"What's really going on here?" he demanded harshly, yanking her into a cruel embrace.

"My sentiments precisely." Richard's lazy drawl, laced with steel, sliced into the tension-filled room.

Sir Robert dropped his hands abruptly, and she swayed to her feet, away from him.

Richard filled the parlor doorway, with Lottie's frightened face just visible beyond him in the dim front hall. Mud caked his hessians, and the wind had stroked his hair into tangles across his brow. His eyes were dark as ebony.

"Byron, it seems you always appear at the most inopportune moments." Arrogance clearly stamped Sir Robert's coarse features. "Mary and I were discussing affairs of the most personal."

Stunned by Sir Robert's audacious claim, she took a slight step back and held her breath. Richard shrugged, almost carelessly, she thought, and strolled toward them. He pinched her chin familiarly and turned a smile of deadly friendliness upon Sir Robert.

"I see. You were discussing Mary's father's debts to you. Really, sir, you needn't fear. There are no secrets between my betrothed and I." His hand stole about her waist, staking his claim upon her in no uncertain terms. "Do you have the notes with you?"

Sir Robert's stunned face showed clearly that he was as shocked by Richard's actions as she was. "I don't carry them about with me!"

"Then let us arrange a time when you will. Say five days from now. At one in the afternoon. We will meet here and discuss the situation. Like gentlemen." Contempt dripped in Richard's final words.

The close, rose-scented air of the cozy parlor sparked with the tension between the two men. Lottie looked from one to the other, as if a duel might be fought then and there. Unable to bear it a moment longer, Mary stepped between them, throwing what she hoped was a beguiling smile up into Sir Robert's scowling face.

"It was lovely to see you again. I shall look forward to your next visit, when all will be set to rights." She hoped her mild dismissal would diffuse the situation. A certain glint in his eyes warned her a heartbeat before he captured her hand, lifting it palm up to his lips.

"I am, as always, your devoted servant, my dear Mary," he murmured with deliberate warmth.

Annoyed more than revolted, she refused to react. Only after Lottie shut the front door behind him did she turn slowly to confront her supposed intended.

His long mouth twisted sardonically. He crossed the room to stare out the window as Sir Robert rode away. "You may not want my help, Mary, but I insist on giving it. That is not a man I want my future wife to be indebted to."

His concern burned through her to multiply her treachery tenfold. "I can't allow it, Richard." She had to protest. "Besides, I don't see any way out of it."

"Of course there is!" He took a step closer. "Two mares are about to foal. They should bring a pretty penny, for their lines are good. Not the bloodlines we will have once Wildfire sires—" His genuine laughter, the first she'd ever heard, rang through the parlor. "Wildfire! My stallion's name is Wildfire!"

His delight suddenly made him look like a young boy.

"Do you remember anything else?" she laughed with him, caught up in his joy.

Pacing the square faded oriental carpet where

only the threads of blue still held their hue, Richard rubbed long fingers at his temples.

"Your uncle reminds me of a man named Jeffries. Now I remember he taught me to ride. Taught me everything I know about horseflesh. He was killed. In the colonies."

Shaking his head, he stopped, a furrow of pain marring his brow as he turned back to her. "That's all I can remember. But it's a beginning."

He stepped in front of her, placing one caressing hand on her shoulder while the other lifted her chin between a thumb and forefinger. "Soon I'll remember everything. I look forward to that, Mary. Particularly I look forward to my memories of you."

The shock of his touch on her face was as powerful, no, more so than it had been the first time. It suspended rational thought; every feeling ceased except the hot stirrings through her veins and the heavy load of guilt around her heart. It was a lethal combination to her burdened soul, his touch and the vulnerable questing gaze with which he searched her face, as if she were a precious puzzle he must solve.

She knew exactly what she was—a liar and a cheat!

Moving away from his silken hands, she swallowed, a difficult task considering the tightness of her throat.

"Yes, soon all your memories will return. I, too, look forward to that day."

It was becoming a habit to stand at the upstairs window to observe Mary undetected. She was preparing for her morning ride. Of late, he'd stayed away. His sleepless nights were forming the pattern of his days. The dark hours found him, wide-eyed, staring at nothing as he forced inroads into his blank mind, searching for any faint memory. He was beginning to see a path, the faintest lightening in the blackness. He sensed that patience was not a virtue he'd ever possessed, but he practiced it now with Mary. He desired her. But for unknown reasons he felt compelled to keep his distance. The kiss, the few touches between them had produced feelings that did not match his fuzzy yet oddly distinct recollections of his intended bride. Had the accident altered him in some way, or perhaps her, so that whatever was between them had grown and ripened?

A wave of impatience with his recalcitrant mind drove him down to the kitchen. Mayhap Lottie could help him.

He found her with the sleeves of her blue merino dress rolled up to her elbows, and she was covered with flour. It flew around her plump hands as she kneaded bread dough, it clung in a white film to her heaving bosom, and specks of it dotted her rosy cheeks.

"Lottie, where has Mary gone off to?" Propping one shoulder against the small fireplace mantel, he watched with tightly reined impatience as she stared up at him, her rosebud mouth uncharacteristically drooping.

"She's off to the pond," she answered slowly, wiping her hands on a fluffy blue cloth. "Why are you asking?"

"I thought I'd join her and bring a picnic. Can you help me?"

For an instant he saw a kind of panic on her face.

Then her kind eyes softened, and her lips curled up in their usual response. "Yes, I'll help you."

She flew around the kitchen, filling a basket with leftovers from yesterday's luncheon and, seeing his longing look, two still-warm apple tarts.

She hummed while she worked, an odd, off-key, tuneless humming, that nonetheless cheered him. It stopped abruptly when he picked up the basket to go.

"Richard, Mary's a good girl. Truly she is."

He paused, and gave her a smile of rare compassion. "Mary is quite safe with me, I promise you."

It dawned on him, as he rode away on Wildfire, the basket carefully balanced in front of him, how odd Lottie's choice of words had been. He might have lost his memory, but there still existed a code of honor which dictated that one did not ravish his intended. He certainly had no intention of forcing himself upon his future bride. He simply needed to understand her and their relationship more clearly to pick his way through the darkness. Today was a day for beginnings. A greater understanding would grow between him and Mary, and that would lead to his answers. Then he could forge a new path.

He found Mary on a lovely sloping bank above a clear waterfall splashing over the rocks strewn in its bed, which formed the pool about ten feet below. A willow tree rustled in the wind, bending its long branches in a curtain around her. Instinctively he knew that this was a secret sacred childhood place.

She'd taken her boots off and now sat with her arms wrapped around her bent knees and her rich heavy hair hiding her face.

"Mary."

At the sound of her name she sprang up. When

she recognized him, the shock in her wide fawn eyes shifted to something that suddenly made the sun too warm upon his skin.

"Richard, what are you doing here?"

"Bringing you a picnic."

He delighted in the rush of color washing her translucent cheeks and the lights of pleasure shooting through her cornflower eyes. He would always be able to gauge his bethrothed's moods by her enchanting blush. As enticing as Mary appeared, as the sunbeams coming through the overhanging tree dappled gold lights into her fall of auburn hair, she was not a woman who he would have thought could wield this kind of power over him. Instinct seemed to be returning first.

How else could he know that what he was feeling at this precise moment was absolutely new?

She helped him spread out a cloth and unpack the basket. Her manner was playful as she set out all the goodies Lottie had packed. But some abstract sense, coupled with a newly recovered instinct, told him that her playfulness was born of apprehension. He was noticing it more and more when they were together. In order to banish it from this day when he was determined to forge a new beginning in his assault against his closed mind, he began to talk.

Although he was rather limited, considering that his mind was like a babe's hatched fully grown only days ago, he touched on subjects that he knew were dear to both their hearts: horses and the land. One thing led to another, until their ideas and opinions tumbled over one another, bringing to life new thoughts and plans, and feelings.

No one thing broke through, suddenly unlocking

his mind, but he did discover what lurked beneath Mary's undeniably lovely exterior. Goodness, as Lottie had said. Wit. And an honesty he found utterly irresistible.

His eyes traveled from her fingers, sticky with apple tart, up the graceful arm to her softly rounded shoulder, on to her appealing face. To his surprise, he found a shadow clouding her eyes.

"Mary, what's troubling you?" He couldn't resist asking.

She rested her chin on her fist and gazed solemnly to where he sprawled on his side, his head on his curled arm.

"Richard, we must talk."

"I thought we had been," he said, holding her in a lazy gaze as he stretched contentedly.

"Yes, but there is something of great import we must discuss at once." A thread of great anxiety in her voice caused him to sit up so that he could look directly into her eyes.

What she saw seemed to confuse her. "You are feeling quite well now, aren't you?" she asked with a particularly plaintive note.

The constant nagging headache he'd been experiencing until this lovely day suddenly reappeared behind his eyes and he blinked, bringing his fingers up to rub his temples. "Yes. Except for this blasted headache that appears for no reason."

At his words her cheeks drained of their rosy color. "Oh, no! Here, let me lay a cold cloth on your forehead. It really is quite soothing."

"No, Mary, I . . ."

Ignoring him, she scrambled down the bank, clasping her own white handkerchief tightly in her fist.

Balancing her bare feet on two flat rocks, she leaned over. Richard watched with pleasure the contours of her soft body revealed beneath the ugly ill-fitting clothes.

Suddenly she tumbled headfirst into the pool. It took him a full second to react, his heart pounding as he leapt up. Her gasp of laughter reassured him.

By the time he was at the water's edge she was on her feet. Sunlight played across her creamy skin, her thick hair flowing across her breasts barely concealing what the thin wet fabric of her shirt so clearly revealed. In a moment her dark spiky lashes danced open, and her eyes met his. Temptation rose to taunt him.

He waded in to her, the water lapping around his boots. Her skin was damp and cool beneath his fingers as he lifted her chin. Her back arched with unconscious grace, bending against the warmth of his hand.

Without any conscious thought on their part, their bodies touched, and he welcomed her cool wetness, but it could not quench the sudden fire coursing hotly through his blood.

"My sweet Mary," he breathed before brushing her mouth slowly. Then again. He felt incredible pleasure in her response. As if embarrassed by his undeniably knowing gaze, she closed her eyes and sighed.

He caught her breath in his mouth, pressing her soft lips to his in a full open kiss. He felt the pull of the water around them and this, coupled with her softly yielding sweetness, made him dizzy with pleasure.

When she finally broke free of his embrace she

was trembling, so he steadied her with hands at her narrow waist.

"I've soaked you to the skin," she whispered, a telltale blush staining her cheeks and flowing down her throat, disappearing beneath her nearly transparent shirt.

Laughing huskily, he dragged her closer and lifted her from the water. "I need cooling down," he drawled with deliberate meaning, and was rewarded with another of her delightful blushes. Today was a day of discovery after all.

Today was a disaster, Mary groaned inwardly, as Richard set her carefully on the blanket. She was without shame! And a coward to boot! Everything she most despised. She must tell him the truth at once!

But she couldn't ignore Dr. McAlister's dire warnings. And now Richard's admission of pain proved that the moment was not at all ripe for her to unburden herself. After all, she must think of his welfare above all else.

She gathered up bunches of her skirt and began to wring them out, trying not to notice Richard on his knees before her. Determined to take the situation in hand, she dropped the hem of her ruined skirt and lifted her eyes to his face.

"Richard, really we must . . ." Her voice faltered, as she realized her mistake at once. She should have continued to ignore him, for his mesmerizing eyes were lit with delight, and his long supple mouth was curled in a smile of such luxurious charm, she literally ceased breathing.

"Another memory returns. I adore the way you lift your chin just so when you mean to be firm with me."

His hands meandered along her shivering flesh, catching her shoulders in gentle palms, and suddenly she was inside his embrace. Their mouths searched for and found each other with a caressing intensity that left her leaning limply against the hard muscles of his chest.

She must stop. Stop this charade. Stop these feelings causing her to lose pace with her breath. Stop the needs spinning shocking delight through her veins, igniting embers of newly discovered desire. They had no place in her life. Particularly with this man, especially when all was revealed to him.

It was that bitter truth which finally gave her the strength to push herself out of his arms.

"We must stop," she said in a husky little voice she hardly recognized as her own.

"Yes . . ." he agreed, but his hands continued to stroke her hair down her back in a slow pattern that made her heart pound so loudly, she was certain he could hear it.

"We must stop. It is late, and Lottie will need help with supper. Isn't that what you were about to say, my sweet Mary?" he asked with a gentle kiss on her mouth, and a tender, almost wistful, smile.

Unable to find the breath to utter a word, she simply nodded.

He stood, pulling her up with him. When he turned away to gather up the basket, she had one brief moment to control the feeling that pierced her heart like a shaft. She feared it was already too late for her.

* * *

The Duchess of Avalon sat quietly as Lord Frederick Charlesworth paced the library with long quick strides.

"Bit of a worry, Your Grace. Long promised he'd be back for Alvanley's card party last night. Don't mind telling you the bets at White's are heavy that he's fled the country." His enormous eyes, a Charlesworth legacy, gazed at her with compassion.

In response she smiled, patting a spot beside her on the brocade chaise longue.

"My dear Frederick," she said gently, touching his hand. "You of all people know that beneath Richard's sardonic exterior there is much hidden kindness. Do you really believe he would simply desert Lady Arabella so cravenly? Or us for that matter?"

"Dash it, no!" he grinned quite openly, obviously struck with her perspicacity. "Then where the devil has he gone off to?"

It was a question that haunted her, and for which she had yet to find the answer. She was saved from attempting by Arabella, who burst through the morning room doors.

Immediately Charlesworth sprang to his feet.

"You here, my lord? It is just the thing!" she exclaimed breathlessly. "Your Grace, I am here to throw myself on your mercy."

"Good heavens, child, what is it?" She had to suppress a smile at the child's dramatic and sorrowful pose—even the ruffle around the neck of her puce walking costume drooped in utter dejection.

"There is a Banbury Fair at Richmond and Lady Sophia Lawton has arranged a party. But my father says I can not attend because I don't have a proper escort. So I thought perhaps Lord Charlesworth could stand in for Avalon once again." Arabella looked hopefully at the duchess.

Although she hated to disappoint her, and was not a whit surprised to see Arabella's much-admired pout, she was forced to shake her head. "I'm quite sure, my dear, that Richard would never attend a Banbury Fair with you. They are not his idea of a good time. And most certainly he would not inflict such a thing on any friend by requesting him to serve as his envoy. Unless, of course, the friend offered." Pausing, she switched her calm eyes to Frederick's rapt face. "Of course, I can not speak for Lord Charlesworth."

"I must confess I have a secret passion for fairs. Particularly when there are tumblers and acrobats." His eagerness to please the beauty was evident.

"Does that mean you'll take me?" Arabella gasped in delight.

He flicked the duchess a look, waiting for her slight nod before answering. "I would be delighted, Lady Arabella," he agreed, and then executed a perfect bow.

"Wonderful! We must be off at once!"

With the briefest of curtsies in the duchess's direction, Arabella was gone, Charlesworth at her heels. At the doorway he turned, giving her a conspiring wink.

His kindness with the child was really quite touching. The duchess, always a woman to grasp opportunity with both hands, began to plot the most satisfying of happenings.

So immersed in these happy daydreams was she that when the door opened abruptly, she was somewhat startled.

"Mr. Bertrand Peabody and Mr. Ian Masterton," Wilkens announced ponderously.

Her gaze passed quickly over the tall, long-faced gentleman in the plain black frock coat, and lingered on the slight redheaded man tugging uncomfortably at his cravat. His resemblance to Jeffries was quite remarkable.

Richard had been on his way to Edinburgh. This man appeared to be as Scottish as their beloved Jeffries had been.

With the undeniable instinct she possessed where her children were concerned, she knew that all her questions about Richard were about to be answered.

Chapter 5

"So you see, Your Grace, the moment Mr. Masterton arrived on the doorstep I immediately contacted my client, realizing the importance of Mr. Masterton's possession of the Duke of Avalon's signet ring. After conferring with the baron I came immediately to relate these tidings to Your Grace. Mr. Masterton *insisted* on being present." Mr. Peabody concluded his droning recitation of events with a peevish whine.

The duchess could hardly believe the tale, but the gold ring growing warm in her tight fist served as proof positive. "My son's memory may be temporarily gone, but he is alive and obviously being well-cared for. This is of utmost import to me." She turned a smile to where Mr. Ian Masterton had taken a stance at the white marble fireplace. "You have my deep gratitude for all you have done for Richard."

Fierce pride blazed from his eyes. "It's me and my Mary who are the grateful ones, Your Grace. Richard—excuse me, Your Grace—his lordship is a right one! Game as they come."

Only by blinking rapidly was she able to hold at bay the tears burning behind her eyes. Had the memory loss allowed Richard to let down his guard with these people? She could only wonder at the girl who might have wrought such a change.

"Harrumph." Mr. Peabody cleared his throat, immediately reestablishing his presence. "As I was saying, Your Grace," he began anew. "My client is leaving immediately to retrieve His Grace and return him safely to you. This is a great personal inconvenience, for the baron does not in any way recognize Miss Mary Masterton, nor has he ever laid eyes on her, or ever wished to do so."

At this last she sensed Ian Masterton's rage boiling to the point of overflowing. Frankly appalled at Mr. Peabody's words and the smug smile on his long face, she stood.

"Thank, you sir; your help in this matter is also greatly appreciated." She nodded her head in obvious dismissal.

Preening, he bowed deeply. "Good day, Your Grace." Straightening, he flicked Ian a hard look. "We will be on our way then."

"No, please, Mr. Masterton," she stopped him. "Could you stay so I might have some more news of my son?"

Ignoring the solictor's gasp of shock, she held Ian's eyes. At his nod, she smiled.

Immediately Wilkens opened the door as if he'd been listening and watching through the keyhole, which no doubt he had been. Mr. Peabody had no choice but to turn on his heels and leave them alone.

"Won't you sit down, Mr. Masterton?" She gave every outward appearance of relaxing back into the settee, but she studied him carefully as he perched on the edge of a deep brocaded chair. "Forgive me for staring, but you bear a striking resemblance to

77

my sons' riding master." She reached in her reticule for a linen square to wipe a drop of moisture from the edge of her eye. "Actually, Jeffries was very dear to us all."

"Aye, I know, Your Grace. Richard thought I was him first time we met. Was this Jeffries from around Edinburgh by chance?" he continued, as if realizing that she needed a moment to compose herself.

Grateful, she sighed and looked up. "Why, yes, he was."

"Aye, that explains the resemblance." As he nodded, his firm jaw softened slightly. "Mary's father, John, was my half-brother. After John's mother died, the vicar's family pretty much had the rearing of him, which is why he was such a gentleman and all. Our father found work at Lord Donnally's estate south of Edinburgh and married my mother. Her mother's family name was Jeffries. Wouldn't doubt your Jeffries was my cousin once or twice removed."

"I think there can be little doubt." Having gathered herself firmly together, she lifted her chin, determined to know everything. "Does Richard recall anything or anyone else?"

The red of his short beard faded in comparison to the fiery color suddenly blotching Ian's cheeks. "Aye, he knows his name is Richard." Obviously struggling with something powerful, Ian stared down at the carpet as he tugged at his cravat. "As for the rest, I be thinkin' it's my Mary's to tell as she sees fit."

Then, there was something more going on. She would never bend so far as to *pry* into her son's life, but he was, after all, without his memory. The duchess calculated quickly. She made her decision and rose slowly, carefully flicking out the folds of her dove gray skirt. "Mr. Masterton, I find my anxiety for my son is too great to withstand a moment more. I must see him as soon as possible. Will you help me?"

"I'm glad you're here to help me." Mary knelt beside Richard in the sweet-smelling hay of Star's stall. It was after midnight and they'd been together, waiting, for several hours.

The lantern hung above their heads on a peg cast an intimate light over them all. Star lay on her side, blowing gently with fatigue as the pressure built in her belly.

He reached out and gently stroked the mare. "Easy, girl. It will be over soon."

There was compassion in his voice. She'd never known a man like Richard; she could never, with her limited experience, have imagined that he existed. He had the power to make her tremble with a kiss; his illness made her frightened with the awesome responsibility of the truth; he astounded her with his adroit handling of Sir Robert Lancaster; and he made her grateful every time she realized how much he'd done for her. Every day there was something new to learn about him.

"I'm sorry Uncle Ian hasn't returned in time." Her whisper hung in the air between them. "I thought we had another week before Star's foal would arrive."

Cocking one eyebrow, he glanced at her. "Are you concerned? Surely you've done this before?"

"Yes, of course." She nodded, wishing to reassure him. "But Uncle Ian always was here to help."

"Well, now you have me."

The sure, calm words cramped her stomach in pain where she kept in all her guilt at this lie that she was living and encouraging Richard to believe. It wasn't fair to him! Weakly, she sank back on her heels, her eyes carefully scanning his face. He was so intent on the horse that he didn't even bother brushing back the heavy wave of dark hair that fell into his eyes. He was very much at home here in the stable. Somehow, that didn't seem in keeping with the crested ring and all that her mother had told her of fine London gentlemen. A tiny pain shot through her whenever she remembered that Richard would be leaving soon, if Uncle Ian was successful.

"Richard, have you remembered anything more about your past?" She could hear the slight edge of desperation in her question.

So could he. He gave her a penetrating look. "No," he said, quite calmly. "You will be the first to know when that happens, Mary."

Star convulsed suddenly beneath his palms, her long proud neck arching upward, her ears laid back flat against her head in fear. This was her first foal, the source of both pride and worry for Mary. So much depended on the quality of the tiny creature about to be born.

"It's time," Richard barked out.

Mary scrambled away, making room as he moved into position to help if necessary. She stood pressed against the stall so firmly that the wood scraped through her shirt, irritating her skin.

When front feet and a nose appeared first she gave one gasp of relief.

"It's all right. There will be no problems tonight." Richard's voice was full of exhilaration.

Star gave one more heave, and the foal slipped out on its belly to the bed of straw and nearly into Richard's waiting hands. The white membrane glistened against its shiny black coat, blurring a blaze just like its mother's on its forehead. Richard turned toward her.

"He has the makings of a fine stallion, Mary."

She reached for a soft cloth and cleared the membrane from its nostrils so that it could breathe more easily.

Relieved of her burden, Star struggled up onto her feet. She bent her head, licking the foal's glistening body, and Mary rose slowly, stepping away from it. Uncle Ian had taught her that the mother derived great satisfaction from drying her foal by licking it. It stimulated the flow of blood, giving the foal strength after the ordeal of birth, he firmly believed.

Indeed, within a short time the foal made motions as if to try to stand. Mary had to forcibly resist the urge to help it.

Without warning Richard's hands were at her waist, gently pulling her back against his hard chest. He must have seen her involuntary movement. Could he hear the pounding of her heart? Could he feel how tensely she held herself so as to resist his tempting warmth? Or was he too involved with the foal's struggle to notice?

Urged on by Star's nudging, the foal stood at last.

Held up by impossibly long fragile legs it wobbled, precariously. But instinct won out. The foal began to nuzzle, frantically searching Star's warm belly with its nose.

Embarrassment and pride warred within her as, at last, the foal discovered its prize and began to nurse.

"We can leave them alone now," Richard whispered, burying his face in the side of her neck.

With legs as wobbly as the foal's Mary fled out into the warm night, which was lit by a full moon and hundreds and hundreds of stars. She could escape his touch and the softly spoken intimate tone of his voice, but not her feelings.

His fingers caught her hand, wrapping it with silken strength. She hadn't escaped him after all. She turned to protest.

Cool moonbeams etched shadows beneath his eyes, giving his face an intent languor. "I'll check in a few hours to make sure all is well. Now I'm going to the pond for a swim."

He touched his fingertips along the curve of her cheek, and she felt her flesh heat under the sweet pressure.

"Won't you come with me?" he asked softly, the drowsy heavy-lidded eyes gliding over her in such a way that her pulse skipped twin beats.

Her life had turned topsy-turvy since the fire.

She swallowed back tears, then stepped away, pulling her hand free with determination, or was it desperation?

His quiet laughter dancing along her frayed nerves. "I take that as a no, my sweet Mary. Then go into the house. You look ready to drop from weariness."

Wordlessly she spun on her heels to obey him. Certainly she was worn to the bone, but not from fatigue! Every nerve ending was charged, her blood pounded; she'd never felt so alive.

"Mary, what's happened?" Lottie gasped, clutching her hands to her bosom as Mary darted through the garden door. "I couldn't sleep, with your uncle away and all. Did something happen to Star?"

"No. She delivered a beautiful black foal." The words came quickly like the beat of her pulse. "Both are doing well."

"Then why do you look so distressed?" Placing a soft hand on Mary's shoulder, Lottie peered at her from round eyes, worry filtering through the green in little splashes of dark emerald.

"Richard was there to help, wasn't he? Will he be coming in soon? I'll fix us all a nice pot of tea. It will be just the thing to set you to rights."

"Richard won't be in. He's gone to the pond." Wrapping her arms around suddenly shivering flesh, she moved to the warmth of the low fire in the grate.

"Mary, what are you going to do about him? And all that be happening between the two of you?"

Mary gave one quick breathless laugh. "There's nothing happening! We just helped Star give birth to a beautiful foal. Now Richard has gone for a swim and I wish to soak for hours in my hip bath. I'll take it from the cupboard in my room. Will you start heating up water?"

Without waiting for Lottie's answer, Mary fled the kitchen as she had fled the stable and the yard. But this unbearable weight of guilt and regret wouldn't go away. She was overset by feelings she didn't fully understand and was too frightened to explore.

By the time she hauled can after can of hot water up the narrow stairs to fill the copper tub, she was truly exhausted. She threw lavender into the water and breathed in deeply of the sweet swirling steam as she soaked.

Even luxuriating in the tub, scrubbing her skin until it glowed, and washing her hair until it squeaked between her fingers could not keep her thoughts away from Richard. She must tell him the truth!

She sat before the fire to dry her hair, but instead stared dreamily into the flames, unformed wishes hovering at the edges of her mind. When his footsteps pounded in the hall, the brush slipped from her fingers, clattering on the hearth. She rose to her feet with the impetuous thought of confronting him with the truth at this very moment. Then she glanced down at her lawn gown and collapsed back onto the low stool. She couldn't appear in his room dressed like this! Burying burning cheeks in her palms, she shuddered, remembering how brazen she'd been already with Richard.

Did she allow him to touch her because she must continue this charade for fear of his health? Or did she allow it because his touch brought a response so deep that she ached with it?

Obviously he touched his real fiancée like this. Bitter sorrow distilled in her veins. It was clear to even the meanest intellect that Richard remembered being engaged because he was in his real life. Was her silence keeping him from resuming that life and reuniting with a woman he loved and who no doubt loved him in return?

Pacing her room for what seemed like hours, Mary struggled to find a way to tell him the truth without fear of damaging his health. Although the doctor's dire prediction constantly ran through her head, she could not ignore the proof of her eyes.

Richard appeared beautifully restored to health. Soon, very soon, she would have to confront him. She only prayed that he might understand.

But, in reality, she held out little hope. When Richard regained his memory he would recoil from her in revulsion. He would return to his world, and she would remain here where she belonged, where until now she'd always been content.

Would that old contentment return once he was gone and the shooting sparks of feeling he inspired within her had died?

That question burned in her mind, along with others. But she had to be fair. Richard's loved ones must be mad with worry. She knew she would be in their place. Hopefully Uncle Ian had found success in London. And, if he returned soon, perhaps he would bring the key with which to unlock Richard's mind.

After reciting in her mind every verse she could think of, and after counting the tiny flowers splashed over her coverlet for the third time, she gave up trying to get even a moment of sleep. Flinging back the cover she sat up. Certainly she was doing herself no good here. Perhaps this restless energy would be better served in the stable, caring for Star and her new foal.

She slipped into her chemise, an old worn-out pale yellow cotton dress that buttoned up the front, and her black slippers. No one would see her, so there was no need to tie back her hair. She let it cascade across her breasts and down her back.

She tiptoed past Lottie's chamber and the sewing room, where Richard lay sleeping. The kitchen door creaked as she opened it. She held her breath, waiting, but no one stirred. The only sound was the tall clock in the front hall chiming four. It would be an hour or more before Lottie rose. By then Mary would have visited the stable and would be safely back in her room, hopefully snuggled beneath the covers in exhausted, forgetful slumber.

Carrying the lantern before her, she entered the stable, being careful to step over the lumber, stored just inside the door, that Richard insisted be used to complete six stalls more than they'd ever had before. "Can't grow, if you don't have room," he'd insisted, and her uncle had agreed.

The barn smelled new. The hay was fresh; even the tack hung from shiny nails. She'd have to work hard to keep it, but never for an instant would she think of giving up her father's dream.

The rustling of the horses in their new stalls was comforting, as was the sight of Star and her foal tucked contentedly together in such a way that was difficult to tell where one began and the other ended. She wouldn't disturb them.

Suddenly her breath died in her throat, and she turned slowly around. There had been no sound, nothing to warn her. She'd simply sensed his presence.

The face that he presented to her, in the shadowed space between the light from her lantern and the quilt spread upon the fresh hay in the empty stall next to Star's, was unfathomable. The beguiling smile was new, and the expression in his eyes was impossible to interpret, even if she'd had the strength.

"I couldn't sleep." She set the lantern carefully at her feet.

"In that dress with the light shining around you,

you look like a buttercup." His words flowed like honey. When he reached out, she took his hand.

"Come, my sweet Mary, rest with me."

He pulled her down upon the quilt with him. Somehow she found her cheek resting against the smooth skin of his bare chest where his shirt lay open. She pulled back, but he held her carefully against his side, the steady beat of his heart beneath her ear.

"Why do you hold yourself back from me, Mary?" His quiet voice was startling in the heavy silence of the stable.

"We shouldn't be here like this. We shouldn't always be touching one another. It's . . . it's not the proper way to behave."

Caught in the throes of an embarrassment so great, she did something stupid. She burrowed her hot face into his bare chest, breathing deeply of his clean male scent.

"It seems to me it's quite proper to wish to be with your betrothed." His hushed laugh was rueful. "I was lonely here without you."

Maybe she was exhausted from the burden of her lie, maybe she was overwhelmed by the miracle of the foal's birth; whatever the reason, her head reeled.

"I never realized I was lonely until you came here." As soon as the words passed her dry lips she regretted them, but there was no taking them back or denying their truth.

He said her name once, a ragged inhalation as his fingers glided through her hair to bring her face toward him. The corners of his lips teased upward into a smile. "Is it proper for me to do this, Mary?"

He tilted her head back and laid gentle kisses on her eyelids.

"Does this banish the loneliness for you too, my lavender-scented Mary?" he breathed onto her lips, before pressing his mouth fully over them.

The hands holding her rocked her gently back and forth against him with a sensuality so potent that she succumbed. Her mouth met his with an eagerness that exploded through her like beams of sunlight.

These feelings were too great for her spirit to resist. Here in the stable, where it had all begun, she would steal these moments. After all, they would be all she'd ever have.

She clung to him, their lips meeting, breaking; then she gave her mouth to him in such a way that small unknown wants settled low in her body. His hands stroked her back with a luxuriating slowness that lulled her into a sweet light-filled world of the senses that was as new as it was wondrous.

His palm slid slowly to cup the underside of her breast, and Mary cried out, spiraling wildly back to earth. It was too powerful—and it was wrong! She ripped herself out of his arms.

His eyes widened in response, and his wonderful hands dropped away.

"What is it, Mary?" he murmured, his gaze searching her face.

A moment such as this demanded the truth. "I'm afraid," she stated baldly, meeting his liquid eyes with as much strength as she could muster.

The strong bones of his face relaxed into a tenderness which gave birth to a new ache inside her. Stunned, she didn't protest as his arms came around to cradle her. Gently, he laid her back on the quilt, spreading her hair out onto the blue patchwork like flames.

Slowly he brought one hand up and, with the back of his fingers, brushed one tear away where it had escaped to tickle her cheek.

"It's all right, my sweet. Rest here with me while we watch over Star as Ian would wish us to do."

Earlier she'd thought his face unfathomable. Now, with this new gentleness sweetening his voice and softening the heavy-lidded eyes, she was dazzled by her feelings. In a last frantic effort at rational thought, she stared steadily into his eyes.

"I shall rest here now, Richard. But you must promise to sit quietly while we have a long talk in the morning."

His lips touched her forehead. "It will be as you demand, my determined one," he murmured, a thread of laughter lacing his words.

Having made the gut-wrenching decision, she closed her lids. Her mind was set. She would tell him everything. He was strong enough to bear it. He had to be.

She fell asleep with his fingers stroking her cheek and sorrow filling the empty ache in her chest.

Tomorrow this dream would end.

Richard awoke with his face buried in Mary's glorious hair. Gently removing the silken strands entangling him, he edged away slightly. Mary lay innocently curled beside him. Her sleep-flushed cheeks glowed with color beneath the thick, straight fan of her red-brown lashes. Her ruby lips, sweetly parted in slumber, were nearly irresistible.

Would sleeping beside her always fill him with this odd mix of contentment and pleasure? Suddenly he knew that this was an entirely new idea for him. Just as the senses of an experienced lover had returned to him, he knew that he never slept with his partners. No matter how long they talked and relaxed together in bed after love play, he would always leave them.

Damn! Was this how his life would flow back into his empty mind, in little starts and pictures? It was happening more frequently, but not fast enough to satisfy him.

Images of a beautiful white-haired woman with eyes identical to his often floated through his mind. There were flashes of scenes on horseback, riding hell-for-leather; then the aftermath of a great battle. Had he taken part in it?

So many questions to be answered. So much to piece back together.

The most perplexing puzzle lay beside him. She'd told him in her conscientious voice, which rose slightly when she wished to make a particular point, that it wasn't proper the way they behaved, always touching one another. The burning question was why he actually felt a *need* to touch her when he sensed that such had not always been the case. Before.

Before. Was his life always to be divided into two distinct parts. Before he was beamed on the head; and after?

Another memory drifted into his thoughts, and he gathered it gladly into his small store.

This one brought such a pang of tenderness that he reached out and stroked the sleep-warm cheek. It was the memory of Mary's voice calling to him in the dark, swirling world of emptiness where he had helplessly floated. He had tethered his will to her soft tones and drawn himself back to the living.

Mary's lashes fluttered once before lifting, her cornflower eyes glazed from slumber.

Slowly they focused on his face and widened to once again resemble those of a wild creature, frightened and poised to flee. Mary scrambled to her knees.

"Star and the foal?" she asked, glancing around.

"Content." His voice low, he knelt in front of her. Drawing her tightly to his body, he brushed aside a heavy fall of hair to taste the warm skin on the side of her neck. "As I am with you, my sweet Mary," he breathed into the shell of her ear.

She pushed him away and jumped to her feet. He followed in one shocked movement.

"I can't. *We* can't. It's not right," she cried in a voice he didn't recognize. Her breath came in frayed little gasps, and her eyes pleaded for understanding, the iris expanding to dull the blue to navy. "We must go into the house. We must talk. Now!"

She swung on her heels, poised for flight.

Stunned by the pain he saw on her pale face, he caught her shoulder. "Wait, Mary."

The movement caused her foot to sink into a hole beneath the quilt. She shifted, trying to keep her balance, and Richard lunged to catch her before she fell.

Overbalanced, they tumbled, tangled together onto the quilt. The force of the fall rolled them onto the straw-covered floor. He cushioned her with his arms, curling his body around her to protect her.

Blinding light exploded behind his eyes. The edge of a piece of lumber scraped the back of his head and down the side of his cheek as he rolled to a halt. He squeezed his lids closed against a sharp jab of pain so forceful that it filled his ears with echoes of the blow.

Light and color rushed into the dull ache. Images of people and places overflowed his mind. Then blackness. Into that void flowed new color and images, all coming together to form one vibrant tapestry.

"Richard! Open your eyes, Richard! *Please!*" The plaintive sweet tones he had heard once before called to him.

Obeying, he lifted his lids and looked straight into her wide, deceitful gaze.

Chapter 6

"Thank the good Lord!" she breathed, tears pearling her thick lashes. "Richard, are you hurt?"

"No." He drawled the single word as evenly as he could against the biting teeth of rage that were gnawing his guts to shreds.

Curling up in one fluid motion, he towered over her and looked around him with eyes that were aware for the first time. "I'm fine," he added softly, studying her fawn eyes for answers.

What a wonderful actress she was! He'd had snares set for him by the most cunning women of the ton, and the ladies of the demimonde were forever at his heels, but never had any of them demonstrated such skill.

When had she realized what a plum had dropped into her lap?

For the first time in this charade she played, she reached out to touch his cheek, her eyes wide and deep navy with fear. "Are you sure you're all right? You . . . you look different somehow."

The touch of her gentle fingers fed the flames of his anger. Holding her gaze, he brought his hand to her throat, somehow resisting the urge to press against it and demand the truth. Why had she lied to him?

If Lottie hadn't rushed through the stable doors at just that moment, he was certain that his rage would have overcome his natural curiosity. As it was, he decided to play the game a little longer.

"Mary, Dr. McAlister and another gentleman have just arrived!"

Lottie's face was a study in color contrasts—her round green eyes were bright as emerald chips, the plump cheeks apple red, but there was a white line around her usually merry mouth.

"Who is it, Lottie?" Mary asked.

"The stranger looks like that miniature your mother left you."

"It can't be!" Mary's voice quivered like a guttering candle.

Richard was amazed at the reaction of the two women. They had faced the fire and resulting work with less apprehension. He strode to the stable door and stared out at the doctor and a rotund gentleman, certainly no one to inspire such fear.

"Who is he?" Richard demanded in what he now knew was his normal disdainful tone.

Mary peeked around the corner, then looked up at him, her wide-set eyes nearly opaque. "I believe it's my maternal grandfather, Baron Renfrew."

Exercising extreme effort, Richard kept his face muscles set. He'd never met the old baron, but he'd heard enough tales of his avaricious nature to see a setup. What a charming family trap he'd blundered into!

"Where's your familial feeling, Mary? Shouldn't you be rushing to greet him?"

She stepped back as if slapped by the thread of viciousness in his voice that he couldn't quite mask.

"I doubt he wishes my greeting, Richard." Her

voice rose as it always did when she wished to be precise, although this time it was laced with trepidation. "I have no idea why he is here now. He's never before even acknowledged my existence."

There was more to this than met the eye, Richard reasoned. And with his wits about him, he was a match for any man. He strolled indolently behind Lottie, who hovered protectively beside Mary.

Two could play at charades!

At their approach, Dr. McAlister nodded his head vigorously. "Here they are, Baron. Good day, Miss Masterton."

"Good day, Dr. McAlister," she said evenly, her eyes riveted to her grandfather's scarlet face. "To what do I owe this honor?"

"What abominable manners!" the baron roared at a space somewhere over Mary's right shoulder.

He wouldn't look directly at her, Richard noticed, becoming further intrigued.

"Won't be questioned like a lackey on the front stoop. Why don't the stupid gal show us into the parlor?"

Richard could almost see Mary's heart stop beating as she stood in silent shame.

"By all means let us adjourn to the parlor, *gentlemen*."

His stress on the last word brought Renfrew's gaze to his face for an instant before the baron turned to follow Lottie into the cottage.

With Baron Renfrew taking a wide-spread stance at the fireplace, Richard was forced to lean against the door to observe. Lottie appeared frightened to death and Mary . . . he wouldn't allow himself to even guess at what was behind her façade. At last the doctor sensed some of the undercurrent.

"Miss Masterton, I believe you'd best sit down while we explain why we've come."

"Cease treating the chit like a lady, McAlister." Renfrew flicked the doctor a sneer. "Being peasant stock, she'll be sturdy enough to bear up under the facts I've come to reveal. She's been lying and cheating His Grace and now she's been caught out!"

An hour ago Richard would have planted the baron a facer, even if he was thirty years older and Mary's grandfather to boot. Even now he had to resist the urge to go to her and draw her trembling body into his arms. His anger with her, however, was strong enough to stop him from taking more than two paces into the room.

Lottie turned from where she stood at the lace-trimmed windows and cried out, "More visitors, Mary. No wait! It's your uncle, and a fine lady with him!"

The parlor doors were flung open. Ian escorted the Duchess of Avalon in, as naturally as if they were old friends.

Identical chocolate eyes met and held. Although he fought to still his natural inclination, surely she could sense the wave of love he felt at seeing her.

"Your Grace, what do you here?" Renfrew barked out. "Peabody told you I'd fetch your boy home."

"I could wait no longer to see my son." She stared at him, her face so sad that it tore at his already battered insides. "Richard, I know you have lost your memory, but I want you to know I am your mother. You are the Duke of Avalon. And you are loved very much."

It was one of his greatest acts of self-control not to embrace her and breathe in her wonderful essence which recalled earlier and happier times.

Richard saw a flicker of confusion on her face before she turned to Mary. "You must be Ian's niece."

His mother's kind voice seemed to soften the icy rigidity that Mary was locked in. A flicker of a smile brushed her nearly colorless lips as she executed a curtsy.

"Dear child, I can't thank you enough for your care of my son." The duchess took Mary's hand and raised her gracefully from the floor.

"Madame, this baggage deserves none of your thanks. It is she who has kept him from you for so long!" Renfrew interrupted, striding forward, still refusing to acknowledge Mary in any way. "The gal's deceitful, just like her mother. And as dishonest and lowborn as her father. She's done her best to get her nasty claws into your son, but I'm here to stop her!"

"*Sir, you are speaking of my intended bride!*"

Richard hadn't meant to defend her, but was driven by some feeling too intense to ignore. He threw an arm around Mary's shoulder and pulled her to him. She shuddered once but didn't attempt to free herself.

Rage transformed the baron's face into tight weasel-like lines.

"McAlister told me what the stupid chit's been about. Good God, boy, the gal's done nothing but lie to you! You're not engaged to this baggage. You're engaged to Lady Arabella Hampton!"

Mary stood as if an icy paralysis gripped her. At last she stared up at him with such raw pain on her face that for a moment he hesitated.

"It's true, Richard," his mother added softly, her eyes studying his own. "Your memory loss has wiped it away, but what the baron states is true, dear heart."

"Your Grace! Baron Renfrew! I must interrupt!" Dr. McAlister sputtered. "Baron, I told you it could have a disastrous effect if you shocked this man's fragile constitution. Indeed it could throw him back into a brain fever!"

Always having had the constitution of an ox, Richard was hard-pressed to stop his lips from twitching into a rueful grin.

Adjusting his glasses higher upon his nose, the doctor peered at him officiously. "Having any more headaches, Your Grace?"

An interesting development, this. And an opportunity for him to play out his own game.

"Only now and again," he drawled. "But I fear one is coming now." It was slightly shocking to discover that deceit came with such facility.

"I knew it!" the doctor cried, casting a reprimanding glance about the room. "His Grace must be allowed to regain his memory naturally and at his own pace."

"Rubbish, man!" Baron Renfrew stuck his vein-ridden nose into Richard's face. "Why the blazes ain't you fuming fire and brimstone at this baggage? Don't you care that she set out to trap you, in your weakened state, for her own ends?"

Put like that, Richard could hardly believe it himself, but he strengthened his resolve when Mary shrank deeper into his side. Either she was the greatest actress of all time, or there was something else going on here that he should know about. He glanced around, thereby catching in the corner of his eye Lottie's frantic effort to restrain Ian. Wishing to put an end to this farce, he decided on a bit of theatrics himself.

He spread his arms wide in a gesture of despair, caught Mary by the hand, and dragged her across the floor to the faded wing chair. Sighing deeply, he flung himself down.

"I can't think clearly, my head aches so."

He kept a firm grip on Mary's fingers, forcing her to remain at his side. She stared at him with the same fey look that he remembered from when he had opened his eyes from the dark, swirling void. He wouldn't easily let her off this hook of her own making. For reasons that were not as yet fully formulated in his mind, he was determined that they would all play the game to its end.

"Then I see only one recourse, Richard." His mother's voice brought his gaze around to her, but he was wise enough not to meet her knowing eyes.

"You must return to London. Surrounded by your own belongings, your memories will surely return as Dr. McAlister suggests. Naturally, and at your own pace."

For effect, he hesitated, letting his gaze wander over his mother's cloud of white hair, dressed softly in a cornet, and the pearl drops dangling from her ears.

Then he nodded. "Yes, that seems an excellent suggestion. However, since I would be among virtual strangers, I can't contemplate going without Mary. After all, in my mind she is my betrothed, no matter what has gone before."

"You can't take her to London!" The baron's explosion shook the delicate porcelain figures at each end of the mantel. "I mean you can't introduce her as your fiancée. Think of the embarassment for Lady Hampton!"

"Richard, the baron is correct that we must save Arabella pain. However, I have a plan."

That tone he knew quite well. It forced him to at last meet his mother's determined eyes. What he saw there gave him pause; he only hoped that she would one day understand why he had to continue this pretence, even with her.

"You cannot, of course, bring Mary as your fian-cée," she continued.

"And you will not pass off this lowborn stable-mucker as my relative!" Renfrew seemed like to give himself an apoplexy.

"However, she can come with us as the relative of a dear family friend." The duchess continued in the same reasonable voice that had guided him and his siblings through the rough waters of childhood, as if the baron had not spoken. "It appears Ian was dear Jeffries's cousin. Mary will stay until all is resolved, however long that may be."

"I can't go, Your Grace!" Mary gasped, vainly trying to free herself. In response, Richard only tightened his grip on her fingers.

"Dear child, I understand the prospect may frighten you." His mother gave her the peculiarly appealing smile that had placed the ton at her feet for forty years. "Ian tells me Miss Barton has been your companion since your parent's death from in-fluenza. Of course she may accompany you."

"No! This won't do at all!" Renfrew broke in again. "Even the unassailable Duchess of Avalon can't foist a . . . a doxy upon society!"

"How dare you say such things about my dearest Lottie!"

Stunned by Mary's show of spirit, when she'd shown none to defend herself, Richard let loose her hand. She didn't appear to notice as she faced down her grandfather, completely unafraid.

"After my parents, your *own* daughter, died," she bit out through white lips, "Lottie and Ian came to help me. There was no one else."

Taking three steps, Mary closed her arm around Lottie's quivering shoulders. "Lottie gave up her millinery shop to act as my companion. I won't have you speak ill of her!"

"Nor will I, you bast—" Remembering where he was, Ian stopped. "Beg your pardon, Your Grace."

"Quite so, Ian." Resting dark eyes upon the baron's face, Richard's mother smiled ever so slightly. "I believe the matter is settled. However, Renfrew, there is one last thing you should understand. I fear *you* will be very sorry should any of these ugly accusations reach my ears, in London or out of it."

Falling back one pace from the thinly disguised fury so pointedly exhibited, the baron shook his head. "I want no part in this disaster. The chit ain't no lady. Never will be, in London or out. You'll all see for yourselves, mark my words!"

No one stopped him as he stomped out, slamming the parlor doors behind him.

"Your Grace, I thank you for your kindness, but surely after all this you can see it's out of the question for me to go to London." Mary cast a tortured look to where he still sprawled in the chair. "Richard, certainly you can see that this has all been a horrid mix-up. I . . . I never meant—"

He raised his palm, stopping her. "Mary, none of this is your fault. You didn't know of my prior engagement when we first met."

"Of course I didn't know then." There was the absolute ring of truth in her voice. Of that duplicity he believed her innocent. But for the rest he had to know the truth, on his own terms.

"But Richard, surely you must see my grandfather was right. We were never really betro—"

He gasped, rubbing his temples, again interrupting her before she said too much. It didn't suit his plan to have her reveal herself here and now.

Sputtering, Dr. McAlister rushed to his side. "I warned you! All of you! This man is fortunate to be alive. Any stress could be disastrous!" Hovering, the doctor peered intently at him. "Your Grace, what can we do to ease your pain?"

"I think it best that Mary and I go to London so I might regain my memory. If she refuses, I will remain here with her and hope that I will, eventually, recover." He finished with a sigh, his eyes shut to mere slits. From the reaction he elicited, he thought, perhaps he should consider a career with Kemble on the stage.

"Mary, I think you should go." Lottie's voice choked with sobs. "It's the proper thing to do. And I'll do whatever her ladyship thinks best."

"Aye, lassie." Ian spoke at last. "You're quality, Mary my girl, whether you believe it or not, no matter what that skimble-shanks of a grandfather says."

"Miss Masterton, as Richard's doctor I must insist you listen to his wise council." Dr. McAlister's head nodded pompously.

"I hesitate to add to the burden of decision, my dear, but I fear I must." The duchess glided across the room, standing in a way in which her calm gaze could move easily from Mary's pale face to rest on

Richard's. Her eyes pierced through his façade to his very thoughts, but he threw up a barrier against the bond they shared. There was too much at stake.

"It appears my son needs you with him in London," she continued, her eyes never leaving his. "So I must join with your family and friends in urging you to accept my offer."

He sensed the moment that Mary gave in, saw it in the firm lift to her chin, and the way she widened her fawn eyes.

"Then it appears, Your Grace, we are for London."

London. Tall row houses of whitewash and dun-colored stone. Great mansions with highly polished brass door-knockers. Flagstone streets ringing under the wheels of carriers' wagons, fine coaches, and phaetons. Street peddlers hawking their wares. Everywhere people.

Her mother had described the picturesque bustle time and time again, along with stories of routs and balls and musicales that had made up her world. A world of ladies dressed in fine gowns and jewels, and gentlemen in satin evening coats. It was a foreign world.

A world, her grandfather had correctly stated, that she did not belong to. Not now or ever.

The very thought of what was ahead made her knees turn to pudding. Dropping down in the wing chair, still warm from Richard's body, Mary buried her face in her hands.

She must go to London with him. And he was a duke! The shock of his true identity trembled along her skin, chilling it, chilling her, until she was certain that a block of ice encased her heart.

And his real fiancée. Mary would have to meet her, face her. After sharing his kiss and his touch. Lady Arabella Hampton. Had Richard held her, kissed her, too? Suddenly the ice block shattered, splittering into thousands of shards, each piercing her. She had to plan—she had to get away.

Richard rested upstairs on the narrow bed in the sewing room, sent there by his anxious doctor. The duchess, accompanied by Dr. McAlister, was safely ensconced at the White Feathers for the night, while Mary prepared for the journey. Ian and Lottie made plans in the kitchen.

She had no choice. She would have to go to London. She was trapped in her web of lies, and there was no escape until Richard either regained his memory and cast her out in revulsion, or was well enough to listen to her abject apology and explanation.

Resigning herself to her fate, she dropped her hands in her lap and shut her eyes, trying to shut out the future.

She only looked up when the door pushed open. Lottie and Ian entered together. Lottie placed a tea tray on the low table in front of the settee and straightened. There was a firm twist to her soft lips.

"Mary, your uncle and I were talking in the kitchen, and we have decided it's time to set a few things straight."

Responding to Lottie's fierce look, Ian nodded. "Aye, lassie. After what that bast—I mean, your grandfather be sayin', it's time for you to hear the truth." Taking a deep breath, her uncle thrust his short beard toward the ceiling. "Mary my girl, Lottie never owned a millinery shop. She was workin' at the Thistle and Sword as a . . ." He glanced at

Lottie. Obviously encouraged by her bobbing head, he continued. "As a cook."

"Hardly more than a bar wench, Ian, and you know it!" Lottie corrected sharply, her cheeks bright as flames. But her eyes rested on Mary's face with a steady determination.

"Mary, my parents were the butler and the housekeeper at one of Lord Ferguson's lesser estates. But I was too full of myself to stay in the service of a fine family. No, I wanted to better myself. So I ran off to London. I did work in millinery shops, for as you know, I've a bit of a touch with flowers. I lost my last position when Madame LaFlore sold the shop. I met your uncle after I'd been at the Thistle and Sword for a year. I fair hated the place."

Lottie stopped for breath, her face flushed with bright color. The cherry red ribbons at the neck line of her dress unraveled under her worrying fingers.

"So when Ian told me he was coming here to help you and asked me to accompany him, I did," she rushed on, as if she must spill it all out. "I came with him even though he never made me any promises. If you know what I mean."

Flushing scarlet from his corded throat to his bushy hairline, Ian whistled through clenched teeth. "Now, Lottie lass, you know I'm not ready to settle down."

"Uncle Ian, please allow Lottie to continue," Mary admonished, casting him as hard a glance as she'd ever given. She was appalled at his inability to fully appreciate Lottie's worth. Really, she'd thought better of him, although she'd never allowed herself to dwell too closely upon Lottie and Ian's relationship.

"Thank you, Mary." Lottie sniffed. "I just wanted you to know in case that hateful man ever confronts us again. But I grew up in a great house, and I know what's proper. I'd be honored to be your companion in London if you still want me."

"Want you! I *need* you!" Surging to her feet, Mary swept Lottie into a fierce hug.

"Oh, Lottie, I must have you, but can you really bear to leave Uncle Ian behind even for a short while?" She whispered this last into the fat curls over Lottie's ear.

Firmly gripping Mary's shoulders, Lottie held her at arm's length. "Your uncle can fend for himself. From the looks of things he plans to do so forever." She sniffed as she flicked him a cold little glance.

Chastened, Ian actually shuffled his feet but remained silent.

"Come, Mary, we ladies have much to do to prepare for our journey. Although what proper clothes you have for London could be packed in a small jute bag!"

With a toss of her head Lottie led Mary from the room. There was such earnest determination on Lottie's face, Mary could almost smile, and her fear receded ever so slightly.

Baron Renfrew stomped into the dining room, spewing curses like a sailor. Sir Robert Lancaster glanced up from the quite excellent lamb his cook had prepared, and enquired amicably, "Baron, what brings you to this godforsaken spot?"

"Your abominable blundering, you fool!" The old man spit out the insult, pounding one fist upon the table so hard that the saucer of mint sauce jumped, spilling its contents out in a sticky green stream.

A man fully used to hiding his true feelings, Sir Robert continued with his dinner.

"I sent you a message that I was working on disassociating Mary from her surprising new attachment."

"But you didn't tell me that the man is the Duke of Avalon!"

Even his iron nerves weren't proof against such a pronouncement. Slowly laying down his knife and fork, he at last gave the old baron his full attention.

"Are you certain?"

"I just spent an hour in the parlor of that cursed hovel with him and his mother, the duchess. She's come to fetch her precious son home to London. He still has no memory and so refuses to leave Mary behind, thinking she's his betrothed. Which she ain't and never has been, for he's to wed Lady Arabella Hampton. The baggage tricked him for her own ends. Tricked you, by God!"

Sir Robert leaned back in his padded chair and spired his fingers, studying the tips. The sly puss. He could almost admire her resourcefulness, if she hadn't put such a clog in his plans.

But it was only one more score to settle when he had Mary where he wanted her.

"Well, well, our naive Mary is more astute than I ever believed possible." Staring up into Renfrew's scarlet face, it briefly passed through Sir Robert's thoughts that the old man might have an apoplexy on the spot.

"What do you want me to do?" he asked coolly.

"If you want to keep earning the money I've been paying you, you'll get yourself to London. Fetch her back here! Avalon's smarter than it's good for a man to be. If he starts sticking his nose into Mary's business, I'll be undone."

Some secret thing flashed through the baron's watery blue eyes. Interested, Sir Robert pushed slowly to his feet.

"What a fascinating observation. Pray tell what secrets about a simple chit like Mary could be your undoing, Renfrew?"

"Never you mind!" he barked back. "Just get yourself to London."

"It will cost you," Sir Robert drawled, enjoying the skinflint's discomfort.

Snorting, the baron reached into his brown corded jacket and pulled out a fistfull of fifty-pound notes. "This will get you to London. Contact me as soon as you're settled somewhere. I'll arrange a voucher on my bank. Just get the chit out of London as soon as you can. I don't care how you do it!"

He threw the notes on the table, spun on his heels, and stomped out of the room much as he had entered it.

Relishing the feel of so much ready cash at his fingertips, Sir Robert smiled as he arranged the bills in neat piles upon the table cloth. It had been too long since he'd been in London. Too long since he'd lived the way he deserved to live.

He laughed out loud, thinking about enjoying it all at Renfrew's expense. His stay would be as expensive as he could made it, and as long. For he was more than a little interested in discovering for himself the secret that Renfrew was terrified that the Duke of Avalon might uncover.

Chapter 7

The Duchess of Avalon's carriage was well-sprung and roomy, even with four occupants. Richard's long frame sprawled beside Mary, as she had chosen to let Lottie ride facing forward. The duchess and Lottie were both asleep, their heads resting against olive velvet pillows.

Mary gazed fondly at Lottie, whose poke bonnet was tipped over her eyes and had ridden down upon her nose. All that could be seen of her face was her round firm chin and rosebud lips. The duchess remained the perfect lady even in sleep, not a hair out of place, her hands folded properly in her lap.

Out of the corner of her eye Mary glanced at Richard. His head was flung back, a lock of dark wavy hair fell across his brow, and his magnificent eyes were closed. Even he had succumbed to the bruising pace he himself had ordered.

It was frightening to see how quickly the sweeping valleys, the quaint villages, the slate-roofed chapels of the north country gave way to the gentler, rolling hills of the south.

Soon she would be in London. Richard would be reunited with his love, Lady Arabella. That was right and proper. After all, she had wished to find his family, to restore him to their care. Then why did the prospect give her so much pain? She could never have guessed that he was one of the premier lords of the land, that he was engaged to a true lady. All of her daydreams and fancies had to be forgotten in the light of the truth. That thought brought a sick ache to her stomach and forced her gaze back to his face.

She found him studying her from under his hooded gaze. She tried to smile at him but was afraid and her lip trembled. What was it about him that was subtly different now? Was it the knowledge she possessed, or had something changed him? Since that moment in the stable his eyes seemed harder and the twist to his lips more sardonic.

"What are you afraid of, Mary?"

His blunt question, spoken so near to her ear, threw her into confusion. His soft warm breath was a distraction, but she would strive to be as honest as possible.

"I've never been far from Hexham. My grandfather is correct, Richard. I don't belong in your London world."

"Your grandfather is a miserable reprobate! Good Lord, where is the rest of your family that he can treat you so?" Although the words were full of feeling the glance he settled on her was oddly indifferent.

"I have no one besides my grandfather and Uncle Ian," she answered briefly, not wishing to burden him with the fear and abandonment she had felt after her parents had died and her grandfather had communicated that he wanted nothing whatsoever to do with her.

He lifted one brow and stared pointedly into her eyes, as if he expected more.

"My grandmother died before I was born," she explained, driven by his unnerving silence. "She was the only child of Sir Charles Grenshaw. She and her cousin, Charlotte, were the last of their line."

"Where is this cousin? Couldn't she have helped you?"

All these questions she herself had wondered about. "My mother told me she married the youngest son of the sixth Lord Fordham and they went to the colonies long ago. My mother lost touch with her before she . . . she came north with my father."

She searched his hooded eyes for some sign of what this shift in his manner could mean. There was nothing in them of the man who had insisted he couldn't go to London without her support. It was hard to believe that only a few days ago she had seen such tenderness in him.

"Richard, what have I done to anger you?"

As close as they sat on the carriage seat, Mary couldn't miss the slight tightening of his mouth as her shaft hit home.

"Forgive me," he drawled softly, almost in the voice she'd come to enjoy so. But his small smile didn't bring any warmth to his eyes. "It must be the fatigue of the journey. Rest, Mary. We'll be in London soon."

With that he shut her out, leaning his head back against a green velvet squab and closing his eyes.

She had no choice but to believe him. Just as she'd had no choice but to come on this journey. Despite her misgivings and the miserable guilt that blighted her days, she had come. Because she owed it to him. No matter the cost, she would stay with him for as long as he needed her. She could only hope that her stay in London would be mercifully brief.

The carriage bowled through the streets of London at twilight, clattering over cobblestone streets, past enormous buildings set side by side, twisting and turning until it entered an area of greenery, where the noise of the city was hushed. Set around a square, enclosed by fences, were mansions unlike anything Mary had ever experienced. Certainly, there was the manor house in Hexham, and the squire lived in grandeur there, but it couldn't compare to even one of these dwellings!

The carriage jolted to a stop in front of a high openwork iron gate under a gas lamp. Within moments, a servant materialized to open the door and place a small step stool for their convenience.

"Where are we?" she whispered into the darkness, expecting the duchess to answer.

"Home." Richard drawled the word, pride evident on his face as he stepped out of the carriage.

The duchess gave Mary her peculiarly sweet smile, then she too stepped out, assisted by the footman.

Lottie's eyes were round with wonder. "Never seen such a place. Lord Ferguson's was half the size," she muttered quickly. "But never fear, Mary. We'll do, see if we don't." With a defiant tug at her errant bonnet, she alighted.

Summoning all her courage, Mary followed. Immediately Richard clasped her hand and placed it firmly into the curve of his arm. Her tired eyes searched his unreceptive features for some softening, some return to the warmth that she both craved and feared in the same breath. Now that it was gone, she felt cast adrift in this new frightening world. Sudden trepidation made her search the darkness for Lottie's reassuring presence.

"They're already inside," he drawled, sensing her hesitation. "Come along." He escorted her through the gate toward the Corinthian portico flanked by Venetian windows and crowned with a fan-vaulted door light.

In the soft light spilling through the doorway stood an imposing personage who was unmistakably the butler.

"Welcome home, Your Grace," he pronounced in such a deep, ponderous voice that Mary blinked up at him in awe.

"Thank you," Richard answered, drawing Mary into the deep entrance hall, which by itself was larger than the cottage where she'd grown up. The ceiling rose majestically two stories above her head, and beneath her feet the floor gleamed with a cream Italian marble.

Lottie's mouth was a circle of awe. Mary, too, was overwhelmed, but she refused to give in to fear.

"We are all exhausted." The duchess smiled, and her eyes, so like Richard's, glowed with kindness. "I suggest we retire and have our supper brought to us. Tomorrow we will meet for breakfast to decide our course of action."

Without waiting for comment, she turned and led the way up the wide double staircase. At the landing Richard turned to the right.

"Why yes, Richard, your apartments are in the east wing. Being in the house has sparked a memory . . . ?" There was a certain note in the duchess's voice that Mary hadn't heard before. She turned, catching the clash as identical eyes met and sparred.

Richard shrugged. "Perhaps so, madame. We will see what tomorrow will bring." He sent a perfect bow among the three women. "My apartment is . . . ?" Lifting a brow, he waited.

"It is the third door on the right. Crowley is waiting for you."

The duchess's stare was unrelenting and, surprisingly, Richard looked away first.

"My valet, no doubt." With a flicker of a smile, he turned on his heels and strolled leisurely down the long hall of the east wing.

Without a comment the duchess continued up the stairs. Mary followed her along a wide corridor hung with magnificent landscapes.

"Your room is here, Mary." She indicated a door on the right. "Miss Barton, you are just across the hall. Rest well; be sure to ring if you need anything. Don't worry about tomorrow; we shall talk in the morning."

She returned the way they had come, leaving Lottie and Mary staring at one another.

"I'm frightened out of my wits!" Lottie gasped, grabbing Mary and giving her a fierce hug. "But *you* belong here. And don't you be forgetting it." With a great sigh Lottie released her.

Mary didn't have the heart to argue with Lottie, whose eyelashes were webbed with tears. She knew she didn't really belong; her grandfather's words were branded permanently onto her soul.

"Now get yourself to bed, Mary." Lottie seemed to gather herself together when Mary couldn't respond. "You look ready to drop. Let me come and help you get settled."

"Thank you, Lottie, but I know you're as tired as I am myself. No matter what the others think, you're here as my friend and not my servant. So please, go to bed yourself."

It wasn't that she wouldn't welcome Lottie, even as a distraction from her own disturbing thoughts, but she needed some time alone to acclimate herself to these strange and grand surroundings.

The bedchamber itself was enormous. She sank into a delicate chair of striped blue and cream, which was set comfortably beside a carved marble fireplace. The cheery fire did much to set her spirits to rights. If only her mother could see her in a room like this. An enormous four-poster bed, festooned with cream-colored brocade hangings, stood on a dais at the far end of the chamber. The cherry furnishings were all graceful and feminine, and were polished to a lustrous finish. The windows were hidden behind thick drapes that muffled sound as well as light. The ceiling was muraled with clouds on a pale blue background.

If she was a bit intimidated, she would only admit that it was her surroundings and not the idea that Richard insisted that she was integral to his recovery.

As promised, a serving maid appeared with a delicious supper of cream spring soup, poached turbot with sides of cucumbers, and tiny green peas. The trifle was delicious but so rich that she laid down her spoon after only a few bites.

The maid quietly went about her chores, tending the fire and turning down the bed, but when she reached for the small portmanteau, Mary sent her away. She could unpack her few possessions easily. Besides, she felt vaguely uneasy that the maid would be scandalized by her lack of finery. She hung her two dresses—an evening gown of pale green sarcenet that she'd cut down from one of her mother's dresses, and a walking dress of blue cotton dimity—in the wardrobe alongside the identical costume to the one she wore—her serviceable uniform of black and white.

She poured warm water from the pitcher into a blue-and-white porcelain bowl and made her ablutions. Then she pulled the lawn nightgown over her head and crawled slowly into the center of the four-poster. Her body ached with weariness, and her mind was numb, with so many conflicting feelings and emotions that she'd never be able to sleep. She lay there, trying vainly to order her thoughts and find a way out of her own foolish dreams.

Richard might say he needed, nay, *wanted* her with him, but his eyes no longer sent that message. They were cold and remote. They tortured her. And more important, she felt the bonds between them disintegrating.

Unable to sustain the pain of such thoughts, she embraced the drowsiness finally overtaking her, resisting only long enough to remember Richard's words of encouragement: "We will see what tomorrow will bring."

Richard awoke to a new day. Strong beams of late morning sunlight slanted through the slits of his draperies to make patterns of light on the Bakshaish carpet.

He stretched and gazed around at the familiar objects that he'd always taken for granted. The heavy dark oak armoir made him smile as he recalled hiding in it once so that he could leap out to terrify his brother and sister, when as children they played at hide-and-seek. The painting of a hunt scene, hung over the black marble fireplace, had been a gift from his mother on his seventeenth birthday. He'd come down from Oxford to discover she'd prepared a birthday celebration. He'd been horrified, for he had been too old and grand for such childish fancies. Now he remembered it with a curl of love warming his chest.

Very cleansing, losing your memory, he decided ruefully. The relief upon its return crystallized down into a deep, abiding understanding of its true importance. He could be almost grateful for the experience, if it wasn't for Mary.

Mary.

The warm feeling in his chest spiraled wildly through every fiber of his body as he lay contemplating her treachery. His first rush of rage had dissipated, leaving only a thin layer of anger, and yesterday, he'd realized that she sensed it. He was usually much better at hiding his feelings. Bloody hell, he had honed his languid boredom to perfection! He was notorious for his saber-sharp wit and sardonic humor. Why did they, now, not fill the sucking emptiness inside him?

The thought of vengeance wouldn't do, either. That had been his first inclination when he decided to make Mary play this out. Found out, she was ready to confess all, but like a moth to the flame that would consume it, Richard fed his pain by refusing to listen to her, thereby insuring her stay within his sphere.

He could be honest about himself and his motives, a trait that his mother would no doubt say saved him from being insufferable, but for some reason, this time, the arguments for dragging this bitter charade out to its bloody end were too complex to articulate.

Without question the baron was a bastard—his treatment of his granddaughter verged on the criminal. In fact, there had been a desperation in his attempt to keep her buried in the wild that inspired further study.

He did not delude himself that he'd brought Mary here under false pretences so that she could take her rightful place in the ton. Mary was here so that he could dissect her feelings as skillfully as she had manipulated his.

And she was here to help him untangle himself from a future marriage that would make both Arabella and himself utterly miserable. He could see that this end would take more than a little manipulation.

He flung himself out of bed and went to the wide desk between the windows. He penned two notes: one to his betrothed and the other to Lord Frederick Charlesworth. It was time to start displaying vague memories of certain events and people.

By way of Crowley, he sent apologies that he would not be at breakfast. Crowley reported back that all the ladies had also had trays in their rooms.

Perhaps they were all afraid of what this day might bring.

Richard, dressed in impeccable buff trousers and a rich chocolate corded jacket, was going through his neglected correspondence when Wilkens showed Charlesworth in.

He was nearly an hour early for their appointment, and his owl eyes were wide with concern as he rushed to clasp Richard's shoulder.

"Long! When I got your note I couldn't wait for

the appointed hour. Word has it you've banged your head and forgotten the lot of us!"

Flicking him a smile, Richard moved away from the desk to sprawl in the deep wing chair. "Like most gossip there is a thread of truth." He laughed and heard a genuine and rare note of amusement. "Actually, I *was* struck on the head and lost my memory. But this morning I awoke and remembered you."

The younger man looked so extraordinarily pleased that Richard felt a strong pang of guilt for using their friendship in the way he had planned. Another restitution to make, along with the one he owed his mother.

"Tell me what has gone on in the ton while I've been away."

Settling back, Richard listened to the usual tales of card parties, afternoons at Gentleman Jackson's, bets on at White's, rabid indiscretions, and brutally boring descriptions of balls and routs. Strange, he hadn't felt a bit of ennui up in Hexham, where he'd had to put in quite a bit of hard labor, helping with the barn and the horses.

He noted with some curiosity the number of times Charlesworth mentioned Bella. Even after his pronouncement that Richard must know that the duchess had asked him to act as escort to the lonely child, she seemed to show up in every one of his stories.

A short time later, the look on the perfect oval of Bella's face, as she rushed through the library door and spied Charlesworth sitting with Richard, was a revelation, particularly twinned with Charlesworth's startled smile, followed by a swift look of guilt.

The rage of the last two seasons blushed like the veriest schoolgirl. She tried to conceal it by fussing with the sea-foam green ribbons of the absurd confection perched atop her golden curls.

"Gentlemen, do I interrupt? I came over as soon as I received your missive, Avalon." She fixed him with a steady gaze. "You don't look ill to me."

"Good morning to you, Bella," he drawled, flicking her a smile.

"I knew it was all a hum!" she declared, folding her arms across the bodice of her exquisite walking costume of sea-foam-green-and-cream-striped satin. The flounce at the end of one long sleeve fluttered becomingly when she cast a dramatic gesture around the paneled library. "You know perfectly well who we all are!"

Sighing, Richard crossed his ankles. "I'm afraid all I remember of you is family gatherings when I was quite young, and you a mere child with ... pigtails, wasn't it?"

She managed to mask her affronted look with one of indulgence before he continued, "Our engagement is still a total blank."

"Oh, pooh!" she shrugged with a feigned pout. "I'm sure it will all come back. There's no rush. We shall simply postpone all our plans until you are quite well again."

From Bella's cheery tone and a clearly discernible relief in her posture, it would have been crystal to even the simplest lout that if that event took forever, it would be too soon for her.

"Lord Charlesworth has been an unexceptionable escort in your absence." She smiled prettily in his lordship's direction, batting absurdly long lashes. "And I hope he will be so gracious as to continue during your recovery, however long it takes."

Charlesworth, not being a particularly simple man, flushed bright red and ran a finger between his cravat and his throat as if his breath had been suddenly cut off.

Richard gave his friend the gentlest look of inquiry he could muster without bursting into a pleased grin.

"Of course, Long, you have only to ask anything," Charlesworth gasped, his eyes stretched to truly alarming proportions.

"I give you my thanks." Richard knew it was time to back off a little—clearly the two youngsters before him were uncomfortable. "And one more request if I may. I believe you're friendly with the young Lord Fordham?"

"Jamie and I were sent down from Oxford together. Jolly fellow, really, although not quite up to snuff yet." He finished sternly, as only the recently initiated can do.

"Perhaps you could arrange for us to meet at White's. Say tomorrow."

"Consider it done! Anything else, Long?" he asked with an eagerness that caused Richard to smile with real fondness.

"There is one more thing. A request for you and Bella." He captured them both in his gaze. "We have a relative of an old family friend staying with us. She's badly in need of a new wardrobe and acquiring some town bronze."

As if on cue, the library doors swung open and Richard's mother, with Mary beside her, appeared on the threshold. The contrast between Mary's blue dimity gown, years out of date, and Bella's modish attire was staggering.

Bella's mouth dropped open, and she turned to him with a visage of horror.

"Her?" she whispered harshly.

At his nod she narrowed her eyes, studying for a moment, then smiled. "It will be a challenge, but I can do it!" she declared.

"Plotting are we, Richard?" his mother inquired placidly, floating into the room.

"Your Grace, Long remembered both Lady Arabella and me this morning," Charlesworth reported with boyish exuberance.

"Remarkable," the duchess murmured, giving him a faint smile. "Also remarkable is your lack of manners, Richard." She turned and gestured Mary forward. "Lady Arabella, Lord Charlesworth, may I present Miss Mary Masterton. Mary is the relative of a dear family friend and shall be staying with us for a time."

Mary smiled, transforming her face and bringing a deep dimple to hover at her cherry mouth. Charlesworth struck a very fine leg in response, but Mary barely favored him with a glance. Her eyes were fixed on Bella. After a moment her wide eyes swung slowly to Richard's face. She looked bewildered and ready to bolt at the first opportunity.

He kept his own thoughts locked tightly away, letting his face give nothing away of his true feelings.

"It is a very good sign that you have remembered your fiancée . . . and Lord Charlesworth. Have you recalled anything else?" Mary's soft tone wrapped around him, recalling memories of the farm and the pond.

Lies. All lies, his mind insisted, and if he dwelled on them, he'd give her a good shaking. Or kiss those lying lips, he admitted ruefully. In truth he could stand for her lie about their engagement, knowing she must have had her reasons. What he couldn't stand was the thought that each time she'd been in his arms, her sweet surrender had been an act.

"No! I recall nothing and no one else!" He ground out the words between taut lips.

Shock was mirrored on everyone's faces. But Mary's was colored with pain. Dragging his eyes away from that pale face, he was caught in his mother's compelling dark gaze.

"It would appear my son is overtired from the journey. Perhaps you should rest, Richard."

Grateful for the excuse, he strolled from the room amidst mutters of sympathy. But his mother's condemning scrutiny followed him. To escape it, he continued to feign fatigue. He dined alone in his room and whiled away the evening over a book on philosophy that he had sent Crowley to the library to procure.

But after a while he just couldn't concentrate, so eventually he threw the book down and began to pace. When his bedroom clock chimed midnight, he realized he'd been at this useless pursuit for hours. There was no danger of running into anyone at this late hour, so he went down to the library for a copy of Byron's *The Prisoner of Chillon*—anything to distract him. Amazed at his own restlessness, he poured himself a brandy and tipped the entire contents down his throat.

He poured another and, swirling the crystal snifter between his fingers, paced to the mantel to stare down at the dying fire.

His plan was well in motion, unknowingly aided by Charlesworth and Arabella, who were obviously already half in love with one another. Once Bella's kind heart reached out to Mary, all should fall neatly into place: at the correct moment he could confess that during his illness he had formed the mistaken impression that Mary was his betrothed, and now he feared that he might never recall Arabella clearly. He would certainly understand her reluctance to go through with their wedding. It shouldn't take too much more to persuade her to cry off, particularly if he continued to encourage Charlesworth's interest. It was clear to him that Bella had no more real wish to marry him than he had to wed her.

He sipped the second brandy, savoring its warmth. The image of Mary burned in his mind: Mary, in a clinging nightshift, leading her prize stallion out of the smoke; Mary, relaxing at their picnic, sharing stories of her childhood.

Lottie and Ian were devoted to her. The countryside admired her determination to make her father's dream a reality.

Those images just didn't fit with the truth or with the lies she'd told him. It seemed nigh on to impossible for him to unravel this coil.

With the toe of one boot he kicked at a glowing log, scattering it into bits of flaming fragments. He cursed loudly, crudely, and at great length.

"Has your plotting run into a snag, Richard?"

His mother's voice dropped into the silence. He spun around to find her sitting, nearly hidden in shadows.

She rose from the lounge, piercing him with her calm, knowing eyes. "Perhaps I can be of some assistance."

Chapter 8

With the barriers down, it was impossible now, as it had always been, to tell her less than the truth.

"How long have you known, Mother?"

"Nearly from the beginning," she answered softly, stepping into the glow of light from the dying fire. "How long before the baron and I arrived did your memory return?"

"Mere minutes." He shrugged, staring into the soft amber in the brandy snifter. "Another blow on the head unlocked my mind as swiftly as the first one had locked it."

"Then you know why Mary led you to believe she was your betrothed?"

His head snapped up at the cool question. He could almost smile at his mother's calm approach. She instantly pierced to the very heart of any problem.

"No." The word burned in his throat, and he took a long drink of brandy to soothe it.

"Logic would dictate that both Lottie and Ian know why Mary perpetrated such a misunderstanding. I, of course, understand your reluctance to question them about Mary's motives. Yet it seems clear to everyone but you that she wishes to explain herself. You must know that continuing this cha-

126

rade is forcing her to keep living this lie, out of fear for your *delicate* health. Do you not wish to know the truth because you'd be forced to let her go? Is it love or hate that makes you so irrational, Richard?"

"Love!" The single sharp word skimmed over the flat silence in the room, faintly echoing off the walls. "Mary doesn't love me any more than Bella does!"

A whimsical smile flitted across his mother's face. "I spoke not of Mary's feelings, but your own. Since I know you are not a vindictive man, I acquit you of blind vengeance. Which only leaves that this charade is a means to buy time until you find a way for you and Mary to be together without hurting Bella."

"Good God, Mother, you of all people should know I do what I please!" He flung the last of the brandy down his throat and then placed the empty glass on the mantel with a sharp little ping. "It pleases me to feign illness, using it and Mary, to end a betrothal that is wrong for both Bella and me! In the course of this bloody mess, rest assured that I shall dissect to my full satisfaction Mary's motives for her actions. Then she can flee back to the wild north, or stay here where she belongs. She is, after all, the granddaughter of Baron Renfrew and the great-granddaughter of Sir Charles Grenshaw. Both are old noble families. She has a place in the ton, but certainly not in my heart!"

The fire's light caught in his mother's dark eyes, making them glow a rich cherry brown.

"Your father before you had it, and now you and your brother both possess a self-certainty which convinces you that the sheer force of your will can make events fall into place exactly as you wish. You know that your brother's spirit was nearly crushed when he came to the realization that his will alone was not enough to save his men in battle. What will it do to you, Richard, when at last you realize that you are not more than any other man? That you can suffer, and are suffering, the pain of misunderstanding and love. Your heart is not immune, as you've always commanded it to be."

"I do not love her!" He bit the words out softly, unwanted emotions writhing in his stomach. "I might *desire* her, Mother. But I have desired many women, and know full well that love has nothing to do with what I'm feeling."

She stared into his eyes for a long moment, then nodded. "So be it. Obviously no words of mine will stay you from this torturous path you have chosen. What part am I to play, then?"

He pushed away all thought to continue the conversation calmly. "Surely we are in agreement that Baron Renfrew's treatment of Mary is abominable. I plan to look into it further. In the meantime, Mary can't go about dressed in clothes that any self-respecting scullery maid would toss into the ragbag. You must convince her to accept a new wardrobe. I've elected Bella to take her shopping."

She broke her pensive stare with a blink. "Very shrewd, Richard. They should be good for one another. Just as Arabella and Charlesworth are made to be together."

His mother's words took him off guard. "Then you agree with my course of action?" he said quickly.

"Certainly I'm not blind to what is going on with Arabella and Frederick. And I agree that Mary should take her rightful place in the ton. I simply believe the way to achieve those objects could be clearer and straighter than the one you have plotted."

"There are many paths to the same place." He threw her most oft-spoken sally back at her with an indulgent smile.

"For your sake, dear heart, I hope in this case it is true," she answered softly as she floated from the room.

Even as the door shut Richard stared into the shadows after her. His mother usually offered rational thought and peace. Tonight she'd stirred to life feelings and emotions he'd pushed away, refusing to believe they'd ever have any use for him. It was all Mary's doing.

Mary of the silken hair and skin. Mary melting into his arms, the sweet taste of her lips, the thrill of discovering the gift she presented—as her slow, unfolding passion stirred him. Was any of it more than a phantom?

He swept the brandy snifter from the mantel, stared down at it for an instant, then flung it into the fireplace.

Damn! Shards of glass twinkled up at him in the firelight. All he would have needed was her honesty from the beginning. Then perhaps . . . ? He clicked the door firmly closed on those particular thoughts. He did not love her, and so he would prove to himself and whoever else might be interested.

He took the steps two at a time, his mind flown with so many threads of ideas and plans that he nearly missed the glimpse of Mary hastily dashing from Lottie's room to her own. At the landing, he moved swiftly away from his wing into the west corridor.

What he wanted to do, he had no clear idea beyond a niggling need to confront the architect of his misery. He knocked boldly, once.

Her door opened slowly. Was she conscious that the faint light outlined her body beneath the fine lawn nightgown as she stood before him, the rich auburn curtain of silken hair framing her face?

There was that clear innocence in her cornflower eyes that banished the cursed thought but couldn't quite still the rage that had led him here.

"Richard, are you all right? Has something happened? Your memory!"

There was no disguising the tension of the fine skin of her face, or the way her fingers turned bloodless as they gripped the door.

Slowly, he unpeeled her fingers from the door's edge, stepped over the threshold, and shut them into the intimacy of her bedchamber.

He carried her hand to his mouth, pressing a light kiss on each small knuckle, and finally brushed his lips tenderly upon her open palm.

"Nothing's amiss, Mary. I simply became concerned when I saw you roaming the halls at this hour." He lifted their mated hands to rub her cheek with his knuckles. "Why can't you sleep, Mary?"

Her eyes widened, becoming like clear water, exposing her soul.

"What is it, Mary?" he said carefully, trying to control the powerful thing inside him urging him on. "Tell me what is bringing you such restlessness?"

He buried his fingers in her silken hair, and with

both thumbs tilted her face up to his to cover her quivering lips in a long kiss.

She dissolved into him with a lavish beguiling eagerness that sent flames ripping through his body.

"Richard, I can't bear it any longer!" She breathed the words against his mouth and pulled sharply away. "I must tell you the truth. I have lied to you from the very beginning."

Silence flooded the room as they stared into one another's eyes. His breath came in shallow uneven gasps. Had he come here for this after all? Could his mother be right?

"I never knew you before the accident. You appeared out of nowhere, saved our horses, and were injured. The doctor feared you would never regain consciousness despite our efforts to help you." Her voice degenerated to a choked whisper: "Sir Robert Lancaster was pressuring me to marry him to pay my father's debts. I told him I could not because we were betrothed. If you did not recover, I was going to use Wildfire to stud and your crest ring as collateral to escape from him." She finished with a long sob.

He stared at her, all feelings concealed behind his stony countenance. "How charmingly cold-blooded," he drawled through a chest squeezed by a vice of pain. "What was your plan if I should, unfortunately, recover?"

Tears streamed from her eyes, cascading down her cheeks. "I couldn't go through with it in any case. I sent Uncle Ian to London with your ring to find your family. Then I planned to do what I am doing now: to beg for your understanding."

"Then everything between us was a lie?" He

ceased breathing, waiting for her answer. He *had* come here for this, forced by unfamiliar feelings and the one emotion he wasn't prepared to name.

"I'm sorry," she said gruffly. "I shall leave tomorrow. I only hope someday you can forgive me."

He jerked her tightly to his body so that she could feel every muscle and bone, feel how his skin burned at her acid words.

"Forgive you, my glib little viper? We will see. But one thing I know for certain!"

Her head fell back as she stared up at him in fear.

"You are not leaving until I'm ready to let you go."

"Why, Richard? Why, now that you know what I've done?" she asked desperately.

"Why? Because I want you here until I fully regain my memory. You owe me at least that much."

Abruptly he released her, and she staggered back one pace. The overwhelming urge to drag her back into his arms and kiss her sweet, lying mouth until she begged for mercy was quickly suppressed. Instead he quirked his mouth in a lazy smile.

"To make matters easier for everyone we shall go on as before. I'd appreciate your accepting any kindnesses my mother offers. She feels much indebted to you for saving my life."

The sneer in his voice brought her chin up, and all color drained from her skin.

"For the rest, we can only hope this ordeal will end soon for all of us!"

Even with her face crumpled in weeping, her beauty touched him in ways as new as they were painful. Escaping into the hall, he sucked in a deep breath. He knew the truth at last. Some of her actions he understood and could readily forgive; others, never! He should let her go, rational thought demanded. But there was nothing rational about the feelings and thoughts pounding through him. His sister-in-law's words, spoken so long ago, echoed over and over in his mind: "When your tiny heart is finally given, I hope the lady crumbles it to dust." At last, it was happening.

Her worst fears were happening; Richard knew the truth and had turned away from her in revulsion. Mary crumpled onto the bed in a fit of weeping that drained her of every tear, leaving her eyes burning and her throat aching with dry sobs. Exhaustion dulled her thoughts, all except one: he knew, yet refused to release her. Why?

It seemed fitting that she should be punished for her lie, being near Richard, yet knowing all was broken between them. Even a chance of friendship was forfeit; the price she must pay. Yet she would do it all again, gladly, if it would help him regain his memory and his life.

She could only pray that her revelation would not cause the brain fever the doctor had warned her about. Richard was so strong that she couldn't believe he could fall ill again. She'd had to tell him, before she'd betrayed everything she'd ever been taught. When he'd taken her in his arms again after so long, and after fearing he never would again, she had given herself fully to the emotions only he had ever inspired. Her feelings for him were so overwhelming they shamed her.

Covering her scorching cheeks with trembling fingers, she knew she'd done the right thing. The only thing she could do. She could no longer lie to herself or the man she loved.

By the next morning she'd buried the forbidden feeling deep, holding her head high as she entered the small parlor where Richard's mother waited. But, seeing Arabella sipping chocolate with the duchess, Mary stopped abruptly and turned to go. She didn't feel quite ready to face her.

"There you are, Mary." The duchess's smile calmed her racing nerves somewhat. "Come in, child. Arabella and I have been discussing a shopping excursion for you."

Shock stilled her hand as she reached for the cup the duchess offered. "Shopping?"

"Yes! We shall begin on Bond Street at my modiste. She is the finest in the city."

She glanced in wonder at Arabella's excited face, then back to the duchess.

"Richard wishes it, Mary," the duchess said softly. "I fear it might upset his health if you do not agree."

Quelling her natural instinct to politely refuse such generosity, Mary added this debt to the one she already owed him. Somehow, someday, she'd repay them all.

She searched the duchess's face for some sign that she knew the truth, to no avail. She must go on as before, even though her insides were weak with regret and guilt.

"Thank you, Your Grace. I will, of course, do anything that might help Richard."

Her simple words brought a shout of laughter from Richard's fiancée. "Mary, you're so droll!" Arabella clapped her hands, sending a speaking look at the duchess. "I'm sure Her Grace would agree with me that, in all the length and breadth of the land, there is no one in less need of help than Avalon! I'm sure he'll order his memory loss away as easily as he has always bent the ton to his wishes!"

Mary was struck at once by Arabella's rather callous view of Richard's illness. How could his own fiancée believe that Richard was such a hard man, when Mary had spied his vulnerability immediately?

"Well, we are off," Arabella sighed, standing up and bending over Her Grace's hand affectionately in one graceful movement.

Bowing to the inevitable Mary slowly rose. "Are you not joining us, Your Grace?"

"I was just telling Arabella I will stay here. I understand Miss Barton has a fine hand with a garden. I will invite her to take luncheon with me in the conservatory so we might discuss the well-being of my flowers."

Touched by this kindness to Lottie, who barely left her room for fear she'd do something to disgrace them both, Mary sent her a grateful smile.

Arabella gasped. "Why, you are quite beautiful when you smile!" Tapping one cherry red slipper, she narrowed her eyes, studying Mary. "With your hair and the way your eyes slant just so, I believe I shall strive for a more exotic look. Come, Mary, we have much to do!"

Mary found herself caught up in Arabella's flurry, and before she knew it they were in front of a shop with a discreet sign proclaiming *Madame Beaudin, Modiste*.

Arabella whisked her through the doorway and into a back room hung with narrow mirrors. Obviously, they were expected.

Madame Beaudin herself, a tall raw-boned woman with ebony hair pulled back in a severe bun, surveyed Mary from all angles as she walked slowly around her.

"Everything is here for perfection." She stopped pacing to purse her lips. "The neck, a quite fine bosom, the narrow waist, the long line of hip and thigh. That she should be clothed in this abomination is disgraceful. Mimi, remove it from my sight at once!"

Mary was overcome with embarassment. She couldn't quite believe the compliments, so she fastened on the one thing that was familiar—the contempt of her clothes. Her grandfather was right; she wasn't fit to be in society.

"What Madame Beaudin is saying, Mary, is that you're a beautiful girl, but your clothing does you no justice."

Taken aback at Arabella's momentary softness, Mary smiled in return. "Dreadfully so, I'm afraid." She was surprised at the other girl's obvious kindness to her. She wasn't certain she'd be so cheerful if her betrothed asked her to help another woman look more modish. She was afraid she'd be overcome with jealousy.

Arabella seemed oblivious to anything but designs and fabric. Bolt after bolt of material was considered for walking costumes, riding habits, morning dresses, and ball gowns. Mary's mind swam in confusion. This wasn't her world. She would never need such clothes back in Hexham where she belonged.

Her attempts to stay Arabella fell on deaf ears. A morning dress of buttercup yellow with long sleeves and a softly scooped neckline, another of a pale peach stripe with two ruffles at the hem, and a third of cameo-pink satin with Spanish sleeves were ordered. Two walking costumes, one of gray, the other soft sapphire, each with a matching pelisse and half boots of kid were added. An emerald green riding habit, with a most fetching hat adorned by a white plume, caused even Mary to nod in speechless wonder.

But when Arabella insisted that the neckline of an ivory silk evening gown be cut deeper to display Mary's bosom to perfection, she called a halt.

"Absolutely not!" she declared, removing the silk that spilled across her body like moonbeams. "I shall have no need of such a gown."

"Oh, pooh!" Arabella pouted, her face as pretty as ever. "I shan't fight with you. All in all, we have done quite well."

"*Oui*, Mademoiselle," Madame Beaudin nodded. "How shall Miss Masterton's hair be dressed?"

Both women studied the heavy auburn locks. The assistant, Mimi, pulled out the pins, and an abundance of hair fell straight down her back to her waist.

"It won't hold a curl. My mother once put it in curling papers for two full days to no avail," Mary offered.

"Then we shall trim it slightly and pile it loosely upon your head with combs. It will drive the gentlemen mad as they anticipate it tumbling down upon your shoulders," Arabella declared with a breathless laugh.

Mimi giggled as she buttoned Mary back into her offensive dress.

Madame appeared not to notice as she smiled at

Arabella in appreciation. "Mademoiselle knows men and what they admire."

"I'm not sure about that any longer," Arabella replied, with a whimsical smile that seemed out of character.

Mary was shocked to see a faint flush color her pale skin. Wishing to somehow repay her kindnesses, Mary tried to diffuse the sudden awkwardness.

"Obviously you know what Richard admires. I'm sure he'll return to normal soon."

"Yes, I suppose," Arabella shrugged with that pretty pout again turning her lips. "I know this reprieve can't go on forever."

Even if stunned disbelief hadn't stilled her tongue, Mary didn't know Arabella well enough to question such a shocking statement. Particularly when its implications sent a soaring joy singing through her veins.

But, just as quickly, sadness followed in its wake like a splash of icy water. No matter what happened between Richard and his fiancée, Mary had no place in his life. Of that there could be no doubt.

"There is no doubt about it, Miss Barton, you are a genius with flowers!" The duchess eyed the stunning creation of roses, an artful tangle of ivy, and lacy stems of pinks that Lottie had put together after they had finished a cozy luncheon.

"You're ever so kind, Your Grace. I'd be happy to help your gardener do arrangements for the house," Lottie offered, as the duchess hoped she would. It was the perfect vehicle to ease Lottie's nerves and involve her in the flow of life here.

"I'm sure he will be as pleased as I am at your offer." She placed her teacup firmly on its saucer and folded her hands in her lap. "Miss Barton, may I ask you a few questions about the time you spent with my son?"

She could see by the tightening of Lottie's soft lips that she was steeling herself to deflect any questions about Mary.

"Was he terribly upset at his memory loss?" she asked carefully.

"At first. Then he seemed content to slide into life on the horse farm." Lottie stopped, considering for a moment. "Knowing who he is now, that seems hard to believe. It's a hard life, Your Grace. And he was ever so helpful. Rebuilt the stable when Ian came to London with the ring."

"Yes, the ring. I have much to be grateful to Mary for," the duchess said, weighing her words wisely. "She appears to be as concerned about Richard's health as I am."

"She is, Your Grace!" Lottie declared with round-eyed fervor. "Why, Mary stayed by his side night and day when he lay in that dreadful coma. Poor soul! Once we thought we'd lose him, but Mary refused to give up hope."

"Were they happy together before I arrived?"

She could sense by Lottie's hesitation that she might have overstepped the boundaries, so she hastened to clarify. "The way Richard leapt to her defense when her grandfather attacked her so viciously indicates deep feelings. It is not usually my son's way to demonstrate such overt . . ."

Lottie blinked at her in what the duchess could only believe was surprise. "Fair couldn't keep his hands off her. Playful he was."

"Richard? Playful?" Shock at her offspring's actions was such a rare occurence that she had to consider these new feelings about him and label them correctly.

"Yes, Your Grace. Mary, too, which is something that warmed my heart, seeing that she is usually such a serious child. Loaded down with responsibility she's always been. Caring for her late father's dream of a successful horse farm, while fending off that dreadful Sir Robert Lancaster's advances, and him urging her to wed in order to satisfy her father's debts." Warming to the subject, Lottie leaned closer. "To answer your question, Your Grace. Yes, in spite of Mary's guilt, she was happy, and so was your son, before you came."

The duchess stared intently into Lottie's round face, and what she saw there caused her to nod. Richard had at last met his match. She hoped that her restless, intelligent son had a vestige of sense left to realize it.

The moment Richard collapsed in a deep wing chair at White's opposite Lord Fordham, he realized that the younger man was speechless with fright. A slight movement of his hand brought a waiter at once, and Richard ordered three glasses of rum punch.

Twirling the crystal between two long fingers, he watched both Fordham and Charlesworth take a long drink.

"I appreciate you taking the time to talk with me, Fordham," he drawled, taking a sip and letting the rum roll around on his tongue.

Young Lord Fordham gazed at him in awe. "Your Grace, before a stable fell on your head you never even spoke to me. The fact that we're drinking together will raise my credit higher than I'd ever dared hope. I'm in your debt!"

Amused despite his knowledge of the absurdities of his world, Richard gave the boy a kind smile. "Actually, I need your help in tracing someone once connected to your family. It is Charlotte Grenshaw, who, I believe, was once married to your late grandfather's youngest brother."

A sandy curl fell over Fordham's eyes as he nodded. "I recall stories about him. A real black sheep. Went to the colonies, you know. Died there young of over-indulgence, so the stories go."

"I'm searching for information concerning his widow. Can you help me?" he asked lazily, not by a flicker of an eyelash giving any indication that this was of paramount importance.

"Of course!" the young man exclaimed. "I'll ask my grandmother. The old gal knows by heart every family scandal in the last fifty years. Loves to drag them out at just the right moment to embarrass us all." A deep flush crossed his face at this revelation. "I'll ride to Fordham Manor right now to talk to her, and report to you immediately upon my return!"

The boy jumped to his feet and raced from the room before Richard could utter another word.

Chuckling, he turned to say something to Charlesworth, but the words died in his throat as he caught a glimpse of a familiar figure from the corner of his eyes.

Sir Robert Lancaster. Here?

"Richard, what is it? Has your memory returned?" Charlesworth leapt to his feet, hovering over him.

"That man in black, just leaving—find out why

he is here, who sponsored him!" Richard bit out the commands so sharply, Charlesworth spun on his heels without question to do his bidding.

He would have gone after Lancaster himself, but he was still paralyzed by what he had learned last night about Mary, Lancaster, and, most importantly, himself.

Charlesworth returned quickly, setting another drink in front of him. He realized, to his chagrin, that he had downed the other without tasting a thing.

"You look like you need this," Charlesworth said with a quirk of his lips.

Richard tossed the entire contents down his throat, then looked up into his friend's face. "It was Sir Robert Lancaster, wasn't it?"

"Yes." Charlesworth perched on the chair beside him and leaned closer. "I was told he recently arrived in London. His sponsor is Baron Renfrew. Does this have anything to do with your business with Fordham?"

Pleased by Charlesworth's shrewdness, Richard met his gaze evenly. He'd do very well by Bella, indeed.

"Yes, my friend. The pieces of a rather complex puzzle are finally falling into place."

Chapter 9

Mary's grandfather's actions were forming a distinctly unpleasant pattern in Richard's mind. Caught up in thought, he had to look twice at the doorway of the card room through which he glimpsed Baron Renfrew himself, to be utterly sure he hadn't conjured him up.

His mother was correct. He was now, and always had been, convinced that the focus of his will could achieve whatever he wished. Such arrogance staggered him, especially now that he'd met Mary and couldn't find a way to set all to rights. Yet a remnant of his old self-confidence brought him to his feet.

"Come, Charlesworth, let me introduce you to Mary's grandfather," he purred, flicking his friend a lazy smile.

The baron glanced up from a hand of solitaire. Scarlet rushed into the puffy face above his dreadfully tied cravat when he realized that they were coming his way.

"Good day, Baron. Are you acquainted with Lord Charlesworth?"

Without ceremony, Richard sprawled in the chair across the table from the old baron. Clearly at a loss, Frederick hovered beside him. Mary's grandfather remained grimly silent, his beady eyes flicking uncertainly between the two men as Richard smiled gently.

"We were just discussing the ball at which my mother is planning to introduce Mary to the ton."

"You're a devil, Avalon!" the old baron hissed, his face quivering. "I told you I'd have no part of this!"

"Sir, your granddaughter is quite lovely. I don't doubt she'll become all the rage," Charlesworth offered gallantly, in a vain attempt to slice through the awkward tension pulsing across the table. At the look of horror draining all color from Renfrew's blotchy skin, Charlesworth glanced at Richard with troubled eyes.

"Freddie, would you mind leaving the baron and me alone to discuss the upcoming festivities?" Richard nodded briefly to reassure him.

"I'll be in the reading room if you need me," Charlesworth responded cryptically. He didn't even bow to the ugly-tempered man who glowered and was so ungracious.

Richard endured, with some degree of enjoyment, Renfrew's uneasy glare.

"The chit ain't no concern of yours!" the baron sputtered, then drained his glass in one gulp. "What the devil are you up to, Avalon?"

"I was just asking myself the same question about you."

Richard crossed his ankles and smiled, so that any curious observer would think they were having a friendly chat, instead of the careful interrogation he had every intention of performing.

"I caught a glimpse of Mary's neighbor, Sir Robert Lancaster, in here a few moments ago. Imagine my surprise when Charlesworth learned *you* had sponsored him. Here, I thought you'd never gone near Mary all these years. Yet you are obviously a close friend of the man who has attempted to force her into marriage and who holds her late father's debts."

"Didn't know you had your lackey snooping for you," Renfrew sneered.

"What an apt description for Lancaster!" Keeping his tone deceptively lazy, Richard leaned closer. "You've had your lackey making sure your daughter and her husband stayed in debt all their lives. You've spied on Mary and kept her buried away, haven't you, Baron? I can't but wonder what you fear from your beautiful granddaughter."

Absorbing a hiss of air, Renfrew surged clumsily to his feet. "It ain't none of your damn business, Avalon. Don't muddle in affairs that don't concern you. You might regret it."

In response to so paltry a threat Richard flung back his head and laughed up into the older man's face.

His lips rolling over his teeth, Renfrew smirked back. "You'll see. Mark my words!"

"Yes, I believe I will see, Baron, everything. You mark *my* words!" Faint contempt seasoned his voice.

Richard's lazy smile still curved his mouth as the baron stalked out. He rose swiftly to find Charlesworth and spent the journey back to Avalon House dodging his perceptive questions. Frederick had been a surprisingly able ally in the aftermath of Waterloo two years ago. Now, Richard realized with a start of surprised pleasure, he had become a trusted friend.

"I'm not quite sure myself what's afoot," he confided. "I'll have a better idea once I hear what Fordham's grandmama has to say."

The unflappable Wilkens opened the front door, and they entered the gracious hallway.

"Where's my mother?"

"All the ladies are in the afternoon room, Your Grace." The butler's deep voice echoed with importance.

Placing a hand on Charlesworth's shoulder, Richard urged him to follow. "Say nothing to the ladies. Just be aware Lancaster is not to be trusted. If you should see him anywhere near Mary you must make it known to me at once."

With a stern twist to his kind mouth, Frederick nodded solemnly. "Of course, Long. At once!"

Satisfied at this day's work, Richard flung open the doors. All three ladies instantly looked up from their needlework. From the comfortable scene they presented, it appeared that they were all in great charity with each other.

His eyes searched for and found Mary's open cornflower gaze. Her glorious hair was piled loosely on top of her head. An ivory comb over one small shell-like ear looked ready to give way and allow a heavy lock of auburn to spill across Mary's smooth throat. There was something oddly enticing about the loose arrangement of hair that at any moment might tumble down around her shoulders and breasts. His fingers tingled, remembering the feel of the silken strands in his hands.

"Your hair looks quite fetching, Mary," he drawled as evenly as possible.

"Do you like it, Avalon? It was my idea." Arabella preened. "What do you think, my lord?" she asked sweetly of Charlesworth, from whom she'd scarcely removed her eye since he appeared.

"I must agree with Long, besides adding my compliments to you, Lady Arabella, on your sense of style. It's quite perfect for Miss Masterton's unique beauty."

His gallantry brought a surprising flush of color to Bella's pale skin, something Richard had rarely, if ever, seen on the spoiled beauty's countenance.

Of Mary's delightful blush he had too many memories to contemplate with any degree of sangfroid at this time or place. To stop them, he turned the conversation to a different tack.

"Mother, I've decided the best way to jog this stubborn memory of mine is to have a ball for all of our friends." He met his mother's dark, questioning eyes with a steady stare of his own. "Besides helping me remember, it will give us the opportunity to introduce Mary to the ton."

Mary's gasp warred with Bella's laughter.

"See, Mary, I knew you would have need of a ball gown!"

Richard wasn't listening to Bella's excited questions or his mother's calmer replies. He was staring at Mary. She rose slowly to her feet, and in her eyes was an expression of utter confusion.

"Richard, I must speak with you alone," she muttered in an almost inarticulate flutter, and bolted through the door.

He caught up with her at the entrance to the conservatory. Lottie was bent over some plants at the far end of the sunny room, so Richard led Mary to the bench next to the fountain whose shepherdess eternally poured water from a pail onto the stones around her feet. The splashing water would hide their voices and give them the privacy Mary sought.

He sat down beside her on the cool bench, his gaze holding hers. Her usually deep blue eyes had the opaque quality he'd first seen on her grandfather's arrival in Hexham. It had been there again last night when she'd finally told him the bitter truth. As a herald of powerful emotion, it was potent in the air of utter vulnerability it gave her.

"Why would you wish to introduce me to the ton? Especially after last night; especially considering how you feel about me," she asked softly.

"And how is that?" he taunted, despite what his instinct demanded. If only he could flow with this fire between them that had been forged in those dark hours, when he lay close to death and only her voice and touch had called him back. A different man had awakened in her arms; free of the constraint of his cynicism, he'd touched and enjoyed the pleasures of life in a new way. But his greatest joy had been the compelling gift Mary had offered, the slow flowering of her passion. He couldn't quite accept the fact that she had only been pretending for her own ends. No doubt such denial was a stubborn remnant of his famed arrogance.

"How *do* I feel about you?" This time he waited for a reply. When it didn't come, he reached out slowly to release the curl from the fragile comb behind her ear. He wound the thick strand around his wrist and tugged gently, bringing their faces closer. "Nothing to say, Mary? No more lies to tell? No more pretending? No more having to endure this?"

A whimper escaped her as his hard fingers tilted her chin. His mouth sought her mouth. The kiss was hot and scarring, spiraling arousal through his blood. Dragging his lips from her, he admitted to himself that he'd wished to punish her, but had only deepened his own wound.

"Are you happy, Richard?" she flashed out. "I wonder which one of us is the more accomplished liar!" Her anger brought full color back to her eyes, and they shot blue flames.

"The man I knew those weeks in Hexham might turn away from me for my terrible lie, but he would never have played such cruel games. Don't make everyone else pay for my mistakes. This absurd idea for a ball will only bring unhappiness to everyone. My grandfather has no desire to have the ton know of my existence, and I have no desire to be known."

He released her completely, her hair spilling from his fingers. "Your grandfather will get exactly what he deserves," he said with dead certainty.

"It appears you want to see that I do, too!" She threw the insult as she brushed past him and fled the room.

He started to follow, then stopped, whirling around at the shuffle of slippers on the stone floor. Totally absorbed with Mary, he'd forgotten Lottie was across the room. Her eyes glared at him, accusing him, before she ran after Mary.

Battered by conflicting emotions, his usual rational manner fled. Indeed, which man was he? The cynical, bored, but always coolly rational, Duke of Avalon? Or was he Richard Byron, a man obviously more driven by his passion than his sense?

The noise in the hallway brought Sir Robert's eyes from the mirror, where he was absorbed in the intricate folds of his cravat, to rest on his chamber door. Renfrew crashed through, looking like the devil.

"Nasty habit you have, Baron, bursting in on a fellow."

The beady eyes, nearly buried in the red fleshy face, flew about the snug rented rooms, surveying the fine furniture and the obviously new carpet and rich bed hangings.

"See you're spending my money free enough. When are you going to start earning it? You stupid fool! It might already be too late!"

Watching the old man's reflection in the glass, Sir Robert smiled. "As you can see, I am dressed and ready to make a call now on my beloved Mary."

"What *you* don't see is that Avalon has already ferreted out I sponsored you into White's. He's on to us!" Ramming his bulbous nose practically into Sir Robert's face, he glared. "He's planning a ball to introduce Mary to the ton!"

Folding his arms across his chest, Sir Robert sneered back. "That humbling experience might be the very thing to drive poor Mary into my waiting arms. Who do you think is going to look twice at the penniless daughter of a man who was hardly more than a stable hand, even if she is the granddaughter of a baron? To overcome such a slur she needs be an heiress."

There it was again—something shifting deep in the old man's eyes!

"Thinking of leaving her your fortune, Renfrew?" he taunted, filled with excitement. There must be something here he could use to his advantage.

"Ain't leaving the chit a farthing of mine!" Lumbering away, the baron paced the room with short strides. "Just get her out of town before this cursed ball actually comes about. Don't care how you do it. Just do it!"

Shrugging, Sir Robert moved away from the mirror and picked up a silver-handled walking stick. "As you say, Avalon is a knowing one, even without his memory. To best such a man might be more than I'm capable of doing."

A greedy man himself, Renfrew had no trouble correctly interpreting the words. "How much to get rid of her now?"

"Twenty thousand pounds a year for the rest of my life." He demanded the audacious figure, and then suspended movement, thought, even breathing, as he waited.

"Done!" the baron hissed. "But I want the job finished quickly, do you understand?"

A hot rush of excitement burned his skin. Good God, his gamble was paying off! There must be a bloody fortune at stake for Renfrew to agree to this extortion. Little did the baron guess that in the end Sir Robert fully intended to have it all.

Flown with success, he managed a comforting smile. "Don't fret, sir. I will accomplish my deed posthaste. Of course I will need some surety of our little agreement." He spread his arms wide in a rueful gesture. "A note guaranteeing payment drawn up by your solicitor, perhaps?"

The look of loathing that the baron flashed him might have discomfited a more sensitive man. Sir Robert met it quite openly.

"It shall be on condition that you get the chit back north where she belongs. Marry her and keep her hidden away."

"Consider it done," Sir Robert bowed with mockery. "And our contract?"

"I'll have it tomorrow," he growled, stalking to the door. "Best your part be completed not far behind!" He flung the words over his shoulder as he stormed out.

Slowly Sir Robert went back to the mirror and resumed perfecting his neck cloth. Even here alone, and to his own reflection, he maintained the outward veneer of coolness. Inside he was boiling with excitement. At last his money problems were about to end! And not just end—twenty thousand a year was a decent fortune. But what heated his blood was the surety, now firmly fixed, in his mind that there was a bigger fortune to be had.

Once he married the chit and left her buried away in the country, he could return to London a wealthy man. Then he'd have all the time in the world to wheedle or blackmail the rest from Mary's unnatural grandpapa. Given what he knew about his soon-to-be-bride, there was no doubt in his mind that he had the perfect tack to take with her.

It seemed to be taking Mary forever to get through the house. She was almost to the safety of the west wing, where she could lock herself in her bedchamber to weep herself into oblivion, when the duchess suddenly appeared at the head of the wide staircase.

"Mary, could I please have a word with you in the upstairs sitting room?"

Good manners dictated that she must nod and smile, even though her face ached from the forced normalcy and her insides quivered.

This was one of her favorite rooms in the vast

mansion. With walls of pale yellow and tall windows that let in bright sun, the stuffed cozy sofa and chairs of chintz glowed in a buttercup light.

Buttercup light. That image brought back, with piercing clarity, Richard's remarks in the stable on their last night together. Other visions flashed through her mind: Richard lying helpless while she held his hand, calling him back from darkness; the first time he'd kissed her in the bedchamber; the golden day at the pond; then full circle back to those forbidden and unforgettable moments in the stable. She hadn't known she was lonely until she'd been clasped securely in his arms.

He'd unlocked her heart and mind to emotions and thoughts she'd never dreamed she was capable of feeling. Was the price of this pain eating away her insides worth those moments that must last her a lifetime?

How happy she was that just three days ago she'd sent for Uncle Ian. It had been for Lottie's sake—she seemed so lonely here in London. Now, suddenly, she saw her uncle's arrival as her own salvation. She'd make up some plausible reason why she must go—and leave this house before anything else could happen.

"I can see your talk with my son did not go well."

The expression in the duchess's chocolate eyes was so full of compassion and support that Mary ached to unburden herself, but she could not add another betrayal to the weight of her past mistakes.

"Your Grace, everything is not always as it appears." Sitting down on an overstuffed slipper chair near the duchess, Mary offered the words as a sop to her need to be as truthful as she could be to this kind woman. "I know you must be aware there were . . . misunderstandings between Richard and me from the very beginning. I want you to know there were desperate reasons for them. I deeply regret any pain my foolishness has caused. I have always been determined to help Richard back to full health no matter what."

The duchess reached out and tightly clasped her hand. "Of course you have. But you are right that things are not always as they seem. I wish you to remember this, and forgive as willingly as you place all the blame upon your own shoulders."

Puzzled by her words, Mary blinked rapidly. The duchess squeezed her fingers once before releasing them to rise and move to a charming painting of three beautiful children. Richard was easy to spot. He towered above the other two: an earnest young boy and a delicate little girl.

"My son is a complex man with many layers that might take a lifetime to explore. But the journey, for the right woman, would be without equal."

Her words concurred with Mary's own feeling in the conservatory. That man who held her with such scalding heat was a different incarnation than the one whose hands and lips had whispered so sweetly over her body in Hexham. Yet in both there was a common thread, a forbidden appeal.

Hardly believing where her thoughts were leading her, Mary rose to confront the duchess. "Your Grace, your son's true betrothed is Lady Arabella. Everyone but Richard knows and accepts that."

"Yes, that is true." The duchess turned from the painting to look searchingly at her. "However, is it true that theirs is a love match?"

Mary couldn't help but remember Arabella's unhappy expression and her words at Madame Beaudin's. Indeed, Arabella did not appear to love Richard, but by his actions when he'd thought her his fiancée, his feelings for his true betrothed were very much engaged.

The thought of Richard suffering more pain and disappointment caused her to be unable to blink back the tears any longer.

"Your Grace, what is it you expect me to do?" she asked carefully.

"I expect you, and Richard, to do exactly what you wish." The calm voice was as firm as it was unhelpful. "In the meantime I wish to express my thoughts on this upcoming ball."

Stiffening her spine, Mary prepared for the inevitable. Surely the duchess knew, as she did herself, and as her grandfather so vehemently reinforced, that she couldn't be foisted upon the ton, any more than pigs could fly.

"I think it an excellent notion, regardless of Richard's true motives. You must know, and believe in your heart, that you have a place here."

The duchess's warmth and confidence called to Mary, making her feel warm and secure.

"Your mother made the choice to live her life out of this sphere. You, too, have a choice, Mary. You must in good part experience both worlds before you choose. I am delighted to give you the chance to do so. In fact, I quite look forward to it," she added, as her gentle fingers settled the forgotten lock of hair securely back into its comb.

She floated from the room, leaving Mary as confused as she'd been after the scene with Richard.

The door creaked slowly open and she turned in alarm. Lottie slipped through quietly. Tiny bits of earth clung to the front of her simple pale pink cotton gown. She'd been in the conservatory, Mary suddenly remembered, and there could be no doubt after one long look into her kind face. She had seen all.

"Mary, are you all right? I came after you straightaway, but didn't wish to interrupt Her Grace." She stretched out her arms invitingly.

Mary stepped toward her just as the door again opened.

"Sir Robert Lancaster to see Miss Masterton," Wilkens boomed.

Another disaster on this day of disasters!

Sir Robert pushed into the room, having apparently followed Wilkens up. The butler gave him a disapproving glance but was too well trained to comment. Lottie stood her ground, but Robert spared her not a glance. He rushed toward Mary. Here, as in Hexham, the brush of his full lips upon her hand sent shivers quivering deep inside her.

"Mary, I came immediately upon hearing of your predicament. Imagine Richard Byron turning out to be the unassailable Duke of Avalon! And engaged to someone else! I'm here to help you in any way I can, my dear."

Falling back a pace from the unpleasant aura which surrounded him, and which always repelled her, Mary lifted her chin.

"Yes, it has been very confusing. The long and short of it is Richard was grievously injured. I am staying here until he is completely recovered. Then we shall see."

"How very awkward for you." Swaying closer, he flicked her cheek with one finger. "This really isn't the place for you, is it? Avalon's sojourn in Hexham

156

was obviously an aberration. He and his family must be eager to put it behind them and get on with their lives. A life that you have no real part in," he said calmly, without a trace of expression.

Mary had borne up as best she could the past weeks, as her confined world crumbled about her feet. She was angry at herself and at Richard, but now at Sir Robert's smug certainty that he knew what was best for her, her pride came to the fore.

The duchess's words rang in a strengthening refrain through her head. Wisdom demanded that she sample both worlds. Truth to tell, despite the pain of being near Richard and at the mercy of his anger, she yearned to stay here a bit longer. She didn't believe for one moment that she'd ever truly be accepted by the ton, but staying just seemed the wise thing to do for the moment. After the ball she would know for sure what, if any, parts of her mother's dreamy memories of the ton held meaning for her. If there was nothing binding her here, she would go home to Hexham, to Uncle Ian. Then she could tell him with utmost honesty, that birthright or not, London and the ton was not her world.

"On the contrary, Sir Robert, I have been made to feel quite welcome." The ring of confidence in her voice pleased her. "In fact, the duchess is giving a ball in the hopes it will jog Richard's memory and also to introduce me to the ton. After all, I am the granddaughter of a baron, whether or not he acknowledges me."

"A ball? How nice for all of you," he said with false civility. "However, given your grandfather's rejection of you, do you really wish to expose yourself to the censure of the ton? They can be utterly merciless."

"Why would they be nasty to a beautiful good girl like Mary?" Lottie's shaky voice broke into the unpleasant spell Robert wove. "I should think she'd be a breath of fresh air."

"Desolated as I am to contradict you, I fear I must." Shaking his head, he strolled toward her.

Sensing Lottie's round-eyed recoil, Mary rushed to step between them.

"You of all people should know about censure, Miss Barton. Just think what a may game the ton will make of your dear Mary once they learn her companion the last few years has been—"

"That's quite enough, sir!" At the end of her tether, Mary exploded.

In mock horror, Robert placed one palm over his heart, and his dark flat eyes widened in surprise. "Mary, you misunderstand. I wish only to be of assistance. That's why I came, to let you know my whereabouts in case I'm needed. I have rooms at Thirty St. James Place."

His gaze slipped past her again to rest on Lottie menacingly. "When you are ready to go back where you belong, you have only to come to me."

Frantic to be free of him, she left Lottie unprotected to step quickly to the door. She flung it open. Wilkens stumbled in, practically falling to his knees.

"Excuse me, Miss Masterton. I was coming to inquire if you and your guest require refreshment."

He was so ponderously proper that it never entered her mind to rebuke him for eavesdropping. Instead she was delighted to have reinforcements.

"Sir Robert is just leaving."

At her pointed look Robert presented a perfect

bow. "I'm sure I'll be seeing you again very soon, my dear Mary."

Alone at last, Mary met Lottie halfway across the room. She wasn't sure who was comforting whom—seeing the plump cheeks smeared with tears, and feeling the deep catch of sobs in Lottie's chest, Mary was filled with rage.

It was more than time for her to seize control of her life.

Chapter 10

Richard had spent the night at White's, tediously keeping up his pretense of memory loss. His regard for Charlesworth was increasing by leaps and bounds. As if the world had suddenly tilted off its axis and was spinning backward, Richard was the pupil and Frederick the teacher. Gently but firmly, he eased him back into the world of the haut monde.

It was doing Charlesworth a world of good, Richard kept telling himself. Besides, when all was at last accomplished, Frederick would end up with his heart's desire. He must keep reassuring himself that this game would ultimately set everyone's life on the proper course. If he didn't, his conscience would burn a hole straight through his heart, or his head, or wherever the bloody thing was supposed to be located!

As it was, after the scene with Mary in the conservatory, his conscience was as hot as coals in a grate. His blazing cogitations, more than the wish to while away the hours with old cronies, had kept him awake most of the night. Riddled with regret and confusion, emotions heretofore rejected by the arrogant Duke of Avalon, he found himself in his library at eight in the morning, pouring yet another whiskey. Frowning, he looked down at the small amount of amber liquid, briefly thought that it was too early to begin imbibing, and promptly tilted the entire glass down his throat.

The door swished open, and he cocked his head slightly to one side, flicking a glance at the threshold.

"Drinking your breakfast, Richard? What a charmingly decadent new habit." His mother, her eyes as bright as buttons, floated into the room, her gray silk gown a cloud of softness about her.

"Yes. Decadent," he drawled. Lowering his lids he peered at the crystal decanter, debating the wisdom of consuming another glass. Finally, sanity prevailed, and he placed the glass back on the tray.

Silk drifted across the settee as his mother reclined gracefully, studying him. "You look dreadful, dear. Aren't you sleeping well?" Her tone held surprisingly little concern.

"Since you know everything that goes on in this house, you know full well I am not."

"Just as I know the true reason why rest is eluding you. Even if you don't," she added cryptically.

The bond of love they shared was only strengthened by the similarity of their questing intellects. For the first time in his life, Richard eyed his mother's placid face with vague stirrings of misgiving.

"What reason would that be, madam?" he ventured, for in truth he could do nothing else.

Her mouth curled in a fetching smile, and Richard's misgiving shifted sharply to forboding.

"Since the grand gesture and the outrageous have always been as natural to you as breathing, it only stands to reason that this momentous occasion could hardly be less. Others might mark the moment they finally met their true match by loving thoughtfulness, as Charlesworth is doing so unconsciously with Arabella. You, my dear, are marking it by dragging us all through the depths of Hades."

He was seized by a desperation more fierce than any feeling he'd ever known to deny his mother's words. "It may not appear so to you, Mother, but I assure you I continue this game not for my own amusement, but to benefit others."

Her even stare of interest spurred him on.

"Given a bit more time Bella shall cry off and I will do the proper by urging Frederick to follow his heart. Meanwhile I'm hot on the trail of the true reason Mary's grandfather is so eager to keep her from the notice of the ton. So you see, I'm dragging us all, as you so charmingly put it, through Hades, for a very good reason." He punctuated his pronouncement with an imperious stare to accentuate his vindication.

"Yes, Richard, I do see." She smoothed the pearl gray silk gown tidily over her knees, carefully examining the delicate fabric. After a few moments, apparently satisfied, her fingers stilled, and she raised a wide gaze to his face. "If I understand you properly, Richard, as soon as you have arranged all neatly to your desire, you will tell Mary the truth about your supposed illness and thus set her free. Do I have the right of it, my dear?"

Mary felt free to push open Lottie's bedroom door after she hadn't responded to the third knock. Her eyes immediately found the white note propped carefully upon the pillows of the perfectly made bed. With trembling fingers she opened it and read:

"My dear Mary, Sir Robert is right. You belong

here but I do not and never will. I care about you too much to cause you any pain. So I'm going back where I came from. Know this time with you and Ian has been the happiest of my life. Your friend, Lottie Barton."

Mary's tears fell onto the paper, blending into the faint moisture stains that already marred the thin parchment. Her clenched fist covered her lips. That horrid Sir Robert and his hateful words had done this!

She wasn't going to let him get away with this cruelty. Somehow, she'd pay him out. But first, she must find Lottie and bring her back to safety. If, as Mary feared, Lottie had returned to the Thistle and Sword, she could only fear for her future.

The thought of Lottie lost and friendless tore at her heart. She was racked with sobs, and her hand shook so that it was difficult to write a legible note to her uncle.

With a commanding presence that was almost as shocking to her as it appeared to be to Wilkens, she demanded that he send a footman posthaste on the road to Hexham with a missive for Uncle Ian. Surely he would be on his way by now, but she couldn't take the chance.

That done, her next inclination was to go to Richard and allow him to shoulder some of this burden, as he'd done in those idyllic days on the farm before reality intruded.

Dismayed and shamed by such weakness, Mary hesitated in the foyer. Wilkens, marching behind her, practically ran her over.

"Are you following me?" she demanded, her nerves stretched painfully to their limits.

"Miss Masterton, you appear to be in a state of

some confusion," he stated with perfect propriety. "How may I direct you?"

"Where is Her Grace?" Her chaotic thoughts craved that odd sense of peace the duchess always inspired. "I must speak with her at once."

"I believe I saw Her Grace enter the library some time ago." Wilkens moved as if to lead.

She stepped in front of him. "I know my way to the library, Wilkens. I need you to ask the servants if anyone knows how Miss Barton left the house. Perhaps someone saw something. Anything!"

He bowed deeply, spun on his heels, and left her. She approached the closed double doors of the library but, hearing voices, she stopped short.

"I repeat, Richard, when are you planning to tell Mary you regained your memory long ago?"

The duchess's calm voice was clearly audible through the wooden doors. She froze in place. He knew? He had his memory intact? She crept closer to hear the response.

"I'll inform her of the happy event when I'm finished with her and this sordid business concerning her grandfather. Then she'll be free to do as she wishes." He drawled the words like a man with an utterly clear conscience.

Reality dissolved around her like melting candle wax. For a moment she felt and saw nothing. When her senses returned, emotions eddied around her—anger, fear, disbelief, despair.

Anger prevailed. It roared through her like the flames destroying her stable on that long ago, ill-fated day they'd met.

She thrust open the door and marched in.

The man whose pitiless nature had reduced the fragile threads of her life to broken bits of string, leaving her untethered to her old existence in Hexham, yet still unattached to anything new, turned to face her.

"No doubt if the truth hit you over the head like my stable lintel did, you still wouldn't recognize it!" She was taking air into her hot lungs in short gasps, but her voice sounded reasonably calm. "Nevertheless, here it is: I heard all that was said!"

"Ah."

The duchess rose gracefully and exited the room while Mary stared into Richard's dark, unfathomable eyes. Neither of them registered the door closing behind her.

"You regained your memory that morning in the stable, didn't you? One moment we were . . . were . . ." Stumbling into this quagmire, she was momentarily lost.

Something flitted deep in his eyes, and his mouth quivered with the suspicion of a smile.

She was filled with bitterness. "You know how we were!" Her power of speech returned in full force. "And the next moment it was gone. Whatever had been between us had vanished."

"How perceptive of you, Mary." His sardonic smile failed to light his eyes, which had darkened to ebony. "I believe the *whatever* you are struggling to name was . . . lust. And, of course your accomplished performance of returning my . . . regard."

"I told you why I first lied!" She flashed out, his last insult scalding her to core. "Once started, I couldn't withdraw for fear it might harm you. But you!"

Anguish fed her energy to whirl away and then back again to face him, as if she must move, do something, to spill out this feeling before it devoured her.

"You've been lying to me for weeks! You regained your memory. You knew I'd misled you about our relationship, yet you forced me to come to London. You allowed me to agonize over your health, your very life, if I should divulge the truth! You're despicable!" she snapped, much like her nerves felt ready to do.

"If I'm despicable, what does that make you?" His smile was so sweetly cruel that he could have been the devil himself, promising forbidden fruit. "I may have continued this farce for my own ends, but my motives are a good deal more high-minded than your charming scheme to steal my horse and my ring even before you had the corpse disposed of!"

She'd expected retaliation, but nothing as cruel as this. "I told you . . . I was afraid of Sir Robert. I had no wish . . . to be forced into marriage . . . with him." Her words came out in sobs of anger. "My only thought was to be free of him."

He strode toward her, stopping so close that she was forced to tilt back her head to search his closed, cold face.

"The debt!" He bit out the words. "Given your amazing performance of loving devotion to me, I wonder how far you might have gone in your scheme to settle the bloody thing. If I'd pressed, would you have given yourself to me, Mary? Would you even now?"

Her nerves quivered like a bow releasing its final arrow. At last, it was too much. All her fears for Lottie, all her pain at the hatred her grandfather showed her, all her love-laced anger toward the man looming over her gave strength to the upsweep of her arm.

The contact of her flat palm against his cheek ripped through her arm, numbing it to the shoulder.

She couldn't believe she'd slapped him. She raised her hand to look at it in wonder, then watched the print of her fingers redden in stark relief upon his white cheek.

His derisive crack of laughter took her off guard.

Before she could push him away, his hands found her waist in a swift movement that jerked her into his tight embrace. The hard knot of pain in her throat made it impossible to speak, and her heart was bouncing so hard against her ribs that she felt it vibrate through her breasts and onto his chest.

She tried desperately to pull away from him, but his arms tightened like a vise.

"Let's find the real answer to my question, Mary." His voice was taut with emotion.

She was too shocked to understand his intent. He took her mouth in a hot open kiss that almost made her lose herself. Only by sheer force of will did she remain standing.

She'd known her own truth long ago, and now she discovered, to her shame, that not even his cruel game could change her feelings.

When at last he let her go, she waited a full five heartbeats before she opened her eyes upon his face, for she feared what she would find.

She looked with wonder, for his strength had dissolved into aching vulnerability. There was a curious imprint of pain in his chocolate eyes. She couldn't believe it. She wouldn't believe it.

She knew she couldn't have hurt him; she didn't

wield such power. Only love, as she knew to her deep regret, could scar the soul so completely.

The door opened, and she stumbled away from him. Trembling, she placed a hand upon the back of a wing chair to steady her knees.

Wilkens's face was a study in contrast; his countenance was a careful mask, but his eyes were nearly starting from his head as they darted from Richard, to her, and back again.

"Your Grace, I am deeply sorry to interrupt." For the first time Mary heard a note of something besides pomposity in his voice. "However, a message has just arrived from Lord Fordham. He must see you at once at Fordham Mansion. His grandmama has accompanied him to town and awaits you there."

Richard scrutinized her from under heavy eyelids. "I must attend to this business, Mary. We will finish our discussion upon my return, you can count on it!"

Mary glared at him as she tried to conjure up a biting retort, but he forestalled her by spinning on his heels and quitting the room.

Then the answer came to her. "I shall be long about *my* business before you return, Your Grace!" she whispered to the empty space.

She sped up the stairs for a cloak to fling over her new morning dress of cameo pink after she had decided that she would rent a carriage and take the road north. Lottie must be on the stage and she felt certain she could overtake her.

The frantic planning threw up a barrier in her mind, protecting her from thoughts of Richard. She gathered a few things, jamming them into her reticule along with her mother's jewelry and all the money she possessed.

When she flung open the great front door of Avalon House, she came face-to-face with Richard's betrothed.

Arabella gave her the self-assured smile of a reigning beauty. "Going out, Mary? I was just coming to see if all your clothes have arrived from Madame Beaudin's."

"Last evening," she said with a trace of impatience. "I don't wish to be rude, but I must be off." Confused, Mary looked both ways down the tree-lined street. "Do you know the direction to a coaching establishment where I might hire a carriage?"

Blinking rapidly, Arabella studied her. "Why, yes. Pulman's—the only place my Mama will ever hire a conveyance—but only, of course, when Papa is out of town, or would be inconvenienced by our taking the barouche. Of course, Mama wouldn't be seen in anything less than the very finest."

Mary interrupted impatiently, "But where is it?"

"Oh, it is quite convenient. Near St. James Place. You have only to send a footman about two blocks north and then west for another six."

"Thank you, Arabella. No doubt the walk shall allow me to fully collect my thoughts," Mary declared with renewed determination.

"You plan to walk eight blocks?" Arabella squeaked in horror, her hands fluttering to her throat. "Whatever for?"

"For a dear friend!" Mary retorted sharply. Giving the stunned beauty a brief smile, she stepped off the portico. Hurrying through the iron gate, Mary was infused with new anger. She, like Richard, had serious business to attend to!

The duchess hurried across the wide entry, seeing Arabella standing in the open doorway gazing out into the street.

"My dear child, whatever is the matter?"

Blinking her absurdly long lashes, Arabella stepped over the threshold. "The oddest thing, Your Grace. Mary just rushed out to rent a carriage at Pulman's on St. James Place. She was actually *walking* there, and without a maid!"

Trying to control an uncharacteristic urge to meddle, the duchess closed the door and drew Arabella into the foyer. "Why wouldn't she come to me and request our town carriage?"

"Well, I must say she looked somewhat distressed," Arabella said, a faint pucker marring her smooth forehead. "Has something unpleasant occurred?"

Unpleasant. The word was meaningless before the powerful conflagration which had, no doubt, ignited in the library between Richard and Mary. And just where was Richard?

In fact, where was Wilkens, she wondered. She could always count on him to know everything that went on in the house.

At that exact moment Wilkens came running from the back of the house. His unusually high color was as odd as his absence from his post at the door had been.

"Wilkens, have you any idea where my son is, or why Miss Masterton has gone off to St. James Place alone?" Her voice, she was pleased to hear, showed nothing of her profound concern.

"His Grace is at Fordham Mansion on urgent business, and it's my firm belief Miss Masterton has gone off to find Miss Barton, who appears to have quit the house for good."

"What?" the duchess nearly shrieked.

It was so out of character that both Arabella and Wilkens turned startled eyes to her face.

"Explain yourself at once, Wilkens!" she demanded.

"Miss Barton left this morning unbeknownst to Miss Masterton. In my opinion, her departure was brought about by certain unkind remarks made by Sir Robert Lancaster when he visited last evening. He's not to be trusted, according to what His Grace told Lord Charlesworth. Since His Grace was called away, I took the liberty of sending for Lord Charlesworth when I spied Miss Masterton bolting."

Arabella's awed expression was not lost on Her Grace.

"Wilkens, how amazing that you could so quickly grasp the situation at hand," the child breathed innocently.

The duchess, who knew quite well how her devoted servant kept tabs on them all, gave him a knowing look. He blithely ignored her, and turned at the sound of the knocker on the front door. With a great sense of self-importance he moved across the hallway and admitted Charlesworth.

"Thank goodness you are here, my lord."

The piercing expression vibrating between young Charlesworth and Arabella was powerful enough to knock one off one's feet. The duchess, however, remained firmly in place as the young man rushed over to take her hand in greeting.

"I received your message and came straightaway. How can I be of assistance, Your Grace?" he asked with boyish enthusiasm.

"You must go to Pulman's on St. James Place and bring Miss Masterton safely home. The child's gone off on her own to find Miss Barton, her companion, who has fled because of Sir Robert Lancaster."

At the soft curse he murmured under his breath, her calm fled.

"Sorry, Your Grace. It's just that Long warned me about Lancaster. But never fear, I shall see to it!"

"Take my coach, my lord," Arabella offered, rushing after him onto the porch. "It is waiting at the curb for me. In fact, I shall accompany you, in case dear Mary needs me."

"Yes, children, go! Both of you. At once!" the duchess urged them, spurred on by a sudden certain foreboding that this dreadful game was rushing to a conclusion that her son, despite his sharp wits, had not anticipated.

Sir Robert Lancaster could never have anticipated such good fortune. There was the lovely Miss Masterton, alone. Without a thought as to why she would be there, he rapidly made a decision. He must and would seize this opportunity.

He tapped the roof of the carriage and instantly it halted. He opened the door and leapt to the curb, practically in front of her. The better to give her no warning, he thought.

She swayed to a halt, her wide eyes shooting blue daggers. A thrill of desire curled through him. Really, the chit was becoming deliciously desirable, of a sudden. His possession of her would be even more than he'd hoped.

To that end he bowed. "Mary, how may I—"

"Step aside, Sir Robert!" For once, she didn't bother with a polite veneer. "It's all your fault dear Lottie has left."

Quickly he looked about the roadway. There was no one he knew and no one who could stop him.

"My dear child, you are ill." He spoke just loud enough to satisfy the few passersby.

Without warning, he gripped Mary's arms with fingers of iron and forced her into his coach.

The door slammed shut and the carriage sprang forward. He leaned contentedly back against the seat as he stared into her pale, confused face. At last he had her exactly where he wanted her.

Chapter 11

The taste of Mary lingered on Richard's lips, and his cheek still stung in tiny pinpoints of pain where she'd slapped it.

Flicking a quick glance into the rosewood-framed mirror in the hall of Fordham Mansion, he saw that Mary's handprint was no longer visible.

The outward signs might be gone, but the wound had seeped inward to permanently scar his heart, or what was left of it after she'd crushed it beneath her heel, he amended quickly.

His honor demanded that he settle the puzzle of Mary's familial difficulties. Then he would have done his duty and paid his debt for the gift of his life, which her care had surely saved. He would be free to put her out of his thoughts and out of his life. Hopefully, Fordham held the key.

The butler pushed open a narrow door, and Richard entered a small room where the fire was roaring. Heat closed in around him, making him deucedly uncomfortable. A tiny woman swathed in a heavy shawl, with a blanket tucked neatly around her knees, sat as close to the fire as possible.

His face flushing bright red, young Fordham rushed to greet him.

"Sorry I couldn't attend you at Avalon House.

Grandmother was too tired to go farther, and she insisted on speaking with you herself."

Fordham's harassed visage spoke volumes; grandmama was a handful. Having successfully navigated the waters with his own headstrong female relatives, Avalon gave the younger man an understanding grin and stepped forward.

"Your ladyship, thank you for seeing me." He performed a perfect bow and honored her with a rare smile, which was free of anything but kindness. "Your grandson told you of my needs, I presume."

Up close, her pale, lined skin showed her great age, but her bright eyes were still clear and alert.

"I see it's true what they say about you, Avalon." She nodded, those sharp eyes doing a slow perusal. "Devilish handsome. Are you as clever as they say, too? That's why I came. To see if you had the answer to the mystery of my friend Charlotte's fortune."

"A fortune, madam?" he questioned coolly. "Could you tell me about it?"

"Of course I can! That's why I made the miserable journey to town!" the dowager Lady Fordham barked out. "Sit down, boy, and hear me out."

Richard sat on the hassock near her, gladly suffering the discomfort of the blazing hearth if she could confirm what his questing mind was already proposing.

She nodded, leaned forward, and poked him with a bony finger. "Charlotte and Peter were great favorites of mine. Although Peter was a scamp." A ghost of a smile flitted across her nearly colorless lips as she remembered. "Most of the family was happy to see him off to the colonies to make his own fortune, since he wouldn't be a drain on the Fordhams. Happy they were! But he died before he could do it. Poor Peter."

A faraway look glazed Lady Fordham's watery hazel eyes. Impatience bit at his nerves, but he slapped it down, waiting.

At length he took her hand, and she blinked, shaking her head. "Where was I? Oh, yes. Peter died before he could make his fortune, but Charlotte married one only a few months after her year of mourning. A banker in Boston, Gallatin, I think was the family name, and they were quite prominent over there. As if that meant anything to me. But Charlotte seemed to think I'd be pleased. Rich as Croesus she turned out to be. And lived like a queen according to her twice-yearly letters. Even if it was in such a godforsaken land!"

With one thin hand, Lady Fordham waved him closer. "Here's the rub. Charlotte didn't have any children. After her husband died she wrote me that she planned to leave everything to a foundling hospital. Then in the last few letters before she died she wrote she'd changed her mind. She was older, realized the importance of family, wanted to leave the money to someone of her own blood. She hit on her cousin, who, like Charlotte, was the last of her line."

The dowager Lady Fordham smiled up at her grandson, who stood as far away from the inferno in the grate as proper manners permitted.

"Maybe Jamie here told you I like to have the know of any scandal broth that might be brewing. Want to know what Charlotte ended up doing with all that money!"

Her long-suffering grandson rolled his eyes heav-

176

enward. "Grandmother, go on with the story. Avalon and I want to know what happened to the fortune!"

His petulant outburst and her indulgent chuckle proclaimed that the young heir was obviously a favorite.

"Don't know! That's what I'm hoping Avalon here can tell me!" She turned shrewd eyes upon his face. "Charlotte died about five years ago. I made discreet inquiries about the cousin. Found out she'd wed that miserly Renfrew and died. Hah! No wonder. There was some talk of a daughter, but she'd disappeared up north somewhere. No one had heard of her in years. Everyone presumed she was dead, too. That's the problem with getting old, young man! Everyone you know dies, and you're left with nothing but memories and gossip."

"Lady Fordham, with a spirit such as yours, you will never grow old." He rose slowly, thinking she was finished.

"Not so quick," she surprised him by continuing. "I thought that was the end of it. Until Jamie came to me with your question. If there's a heiress to Charlotte's fortune, wouldn't mind sending Jamie after her scent."

"Good God, Grandmother! I'm a long way from wishing to be leg-shackled!"

The look of horror on his young face was so comical that it brought a twitch of a smile to Richard's mouth. The humor was not enough, however, to suppress the deadly rage that had grown with each word she spoke.

"Madam, you have saved me weeks of inquiries." He stepped away from the heat, grateful to be able

177

to stretch his legs. He bowed. "In appreciation, I must tell you there is indeed an heiress."

"Ah!" she exclaimed. "I can see by your face how lays the land. The heiress is already spoken for, hey, Avalon?"

Meeting her bright eyes with a steady gaze, he answered reflectively. "That is a question which is still unanswered. Rest assured I plan to get to the bottom of this puzzle. Good day."

Fordham quickly opened the door for him. A welcome draft of cool air from the hall washed over them.

"Glad to be of help, Avalon. Any time!" the boy offered eagerly.

The burden of being a ton leader had never seemed more rewarding as he clasped Fordham's shoulder. "You've done well. Call upon me next week, and I'll let you know how it all turns out."

The image of young Lord Fordham's pleasant features, set in a stunned smile of bliss, could almost offset the unpleasant task before him.

Baron Renfrew's house on Belgrave Square was as squat and unattractive as the man himself. His butler, stoop-shouldered and weary, led Richard into a large room with walls of glass-enclosed bookcases separated at precise intervals by classical statues.

When the butler left to find the baron, Richard glanced curiously around. On the fireplace wall were hung two enormous paintings. He recognized the artists and the value of the canvases. The marble statuary, books, and collectibles displayed must have taken a lifetime and a fortune to amass.

He stiffened as the latch clicked behind him. Slowly he turned to face Baron Renfrew, who was dressed in a black morning coat, with his cravat an untidy heap of cloth about his thick neck.

The baron did not appear pleased to see him. Without issuing a greeting, he seated himself in a wine-colored leather armchair.

"What do you want?" he finally growled with ill-concealed rudeness.

"I want your granddaughter's rightful fortune."

The baron lifted one disbelieving eyebrow.

"The one left to her by your wife's cousin, Charlotte," Richard spat out with equal rudeness. "Your thievery is at an end!

"How dare you!" His jaw quivering with rage, Renfrew exploded out of the chair. "I won't stand for such insults in my own home."

A man known for his languishing boredom, Richard surprised even himself with the speed at which he crossed the floor to place his palm flat on the baron's barrel chest and back him up against the nearest bookcase.

"My God, man! You practically put me through the glass!" Renfrew sputtered, fear in his beady dark eyes.

"Only by exercising amazing restraint am I able to stop myself," Richard replied in a surprisingly even tone, given the scope of his feelings. "My solicitor would have unearthed the whole sordid affair soon enough. But I have inside information. How did you imagine you could conceal this forever?" He took his hand away from Renfrew to pound it threateningly into his other palm. "I for one think you should swing on the gallows for what you've done. But I'll bow to Mary's finer sensibilities," he lied easily. "If you confess all now, she might not have you prosecuted."

Horror transformed Renfrew's saggy skin to a trembling fleshy mask. "I'm a peer of the realm! No one would believe the girl."

"A very small fish in a large pond." Richard spared the man a vaguely sardonic smile. "I hate to sound unduly vain, but I feel honor-bound to remind you of the fact that, given any dispute involving your word against mine, I'd win easily."

"Damn you to hell!" Renfrew cried, his eyes glittering crazily in the dim light. "I knew when I saw you in Hexham that you'd ruin me!"

"Talk. Now!" Richard took one step backward. "What did you tell Charlotte's American solicitor when he contacted you?"

"I told them my wife and daughter were dead and my grandchild was underage and simple to boot. Since I was her guardian, all the funds were to be administered through me." His complexion ashen, Renfrew bared his teeth in a tight smile. "The chit was underage until last year, so I'm not as black as you'd paint me."

"You miserable excuse for a man!" The baron's head nearly cracked the glass, as he jerked back under the weight of Richard's hand at his throat. "Mary was working harder than a scullery maid while you fattened your coffers at her expense. Not to mention the fact that Charlotte died *five years ago*! Since then you've done nothing less than steal from your own flesh and blood!"

Repulsed beyond words, he dropped his hands, feeling sullied by even breathing the same air as this foul creature.

"What are you going to do?" the baron gasped, dragging his ruined cravat from his throat and exposing the imprint of Richard's fingers against the flaccid neck.

"I will have my solicitor contact the legal council in Boston to get the record straight. I will expect full restitution of the entire amount, with interest, available to Mary on demand." He seared the baron's pale face with his gaze. "You will leave town. Permanently. In fact, I'd suggest you might want to leave the country, once this story gets about. If you ever set foot in London again, I'll take great pleasure in making sure you regret it."

"Damn you!" the baron screamed at him. A vein throbbed alarmingly at his temple, and his skin turned a harsh purplish red. "You'd ruin me for a chit hardly fit to do more than clean your soiled linens! If you want the wench, take her to your bed! Don't needs made her an heiress to be worthy enough to ride under the vaunted Duke of Avalon!"

Before he could think, Richard raised his fist to smash the baron's face in, but the old man crumbled into a ruin, weeping. He'd done enough damage by depriving the old miser of Mary's wealth, a staggering blow to a man of his ilk. He needn't pummel him as well, he decided, dropping his arm, although he still clenched his fists tightly to his sides.

"Get your miserable carcass out of my sight," he bit out through tight lips. "If you are still in residence tomorrow I bloody well will call in the magistrate!"

Richard stalked out, anxious to breathe air not fouled by Renfrew. He stood in the center of Belgrave Square, taking in great deep gulps of oxygen.

This day had been a series of shocking discoveries. First Mary had discovered his deceit, and now she would be informed that she was a great heiress. What would she do about it? What choice would she make, now that anything she wished would be available to her? Unaccountably eager to see her again after the emotional confrontation between them, Richard made straight for home.

Wilkens stood in the doorway wringing his hands. Richard ran up the last few steps as if the hounds of hell were after him. He'd never seen Wilkens lose his composure in thirty-five years!

"My God, Wilkens, what's happened! Has something happened to Mary?" Shocked by the strength and direction of his feelings, Richard stood frozen to the front stoop.

"Your Grace, I've left messages for you all over town." Wilkens's strong voice quivered at the edges. "It appears Sir Robert Lancaster has run off with Miss Masterton. Lord Charlesworth and Lady Arabella saw him force her into a carriage. They sent word back they were following them on the road north out of town. But the worst is to come. Upon hearing the news your mother demanded a carriage and followed, by herself."

Questions crowded into his mind, but he didn't waste breath asking them. Coolly, he issued orders. "Bring Wildfire around at once! Then order a bag packed for my mother and Miss Masterton. Have their maids follow in a carriage with Crowley."

He hardly had the words out before he was in the saddle, his great stallion quivering eagerly beneath him. He thundered off to the North Road.

Chapter 12

It had all started this very same way. On Wildfire he'd ventured forth to find answers to questions haunting his restless intellect. Instead he'd found something he'd thought impossible in this world, or any other. A woman who truly touched his heart. *Touched!* What a paltry word for the emotions Mary inspired!

Spurring Wildfire on, he gave one bark of laughter. His famed arrogance tamed at last, and by a mere slip of a girl! He'd learned so much these past weeks in her company. But there had remained still a spark of vanity that convinced him that he could win her on his own terms. Now, as he galloped north, that spark flickered and died. He cared nothing for himself. He only knew he had to protect Mary. He had to save her. And after, well, after, was a different story altogether.

London streets flew by in a blur, as the carriage thundered roughly over the cobblestones. She was his prisoner. How had she allowed this to happen? The moment she saw him she should have bolted. Assessing the chances for escape, she rapidly came to the conclusion that she must hide all signs of the panic shredding her insides. She tilted her face forward to search Sir Robert's shadowed eyes.

"Where are you taking me?"

"Haven't I always stood as your good friend and neighbor, Mary? I am here only to do your bidding. Surely you have some notion where Miss Barton has fled," he said smoothly, his face still utterly free of emotion.

"The Thistle and Sword, on the road to Scotland," she replied as he had obviously hoped she would. At this point, it seemed the most prudent idea to go along with his pretence. She must buy time to discover a course of action. Sir Robert couldn't really be kidnapping her! For what purpose? What could possibly motivate him?

She'd never fully understood his desire to wed her. She might know little of men, but she'd always known that Sir Robert possessed no soft emotions for her, nor did he even hold her in any great regard.

Once, she'd known little of men, she amended quickly.

Every scorching memory of Richard flowed through her mind and heart, but paramount was the vision of the vulnerability on his face alongside her handprint marring his strong cheek muscles.

She closed her lids against that pain, her breath a ragged intake of air.

"My dear Mary."

The touch of Sir Robert's arm about her shoulder and his breath against her ear got her attention. Her eyes flew open to find that he'd shifted to her side of the coach and had his arm resting along the seat back, his fingers just touching her.

"My dear Mary, you mustn't be overset. I'm here now and will handle all for you."

His oily voice infused a new vitality into her sagging spirits, and she resettled herself in a more commanding posture.

"Certainly we won't reach the Thistle and Sword before nightfall?"

"But of course we will!" He widened his cold eyes in mock horror. "Certainly you don't think I'd besmirch your reputation by spending the night unescorted with you? We'll press on until we find Lottie, no matter what it takes."

The destination he had in mind, Mary was quite sure, had nothing to do with Lottie and everything to do with some insane plan lurking behind his unemotional eyes.

She wasn't foolish enough to attempt a leap to freedom from the moving coach. Her only recourse was to get out of this vehicle and away from him, as quickly as possible. She fought off panic and considered how that might be accomplished.

After an hour had gone by she said, "Sir Robert, you know I'm desperate to reach dear Lottie. However, I must ask we stop at the next inn." She felt her cheeks growing crimson but forced her voice on. "I must use the convenience."

He blinked once, his gaze flicking over her face. She hadn't attempted to feign illness from the bouncing coach, for he probably would have simply pulled to the side of the road and opened the door for her to lean out. Perhaps she had lulled him into a false sense of security. In any case, for this request he would have to display a modicum of decency.

He finally nodded. "Of course, Mary. We will be at the Hare and Hound within the hour."

The thought of escape sustained her, making it possible to endure his hateful presence. To hide her fear she closed her eyes, pretending to sleep so that she wouldn't have to make conversation with the monster.

The Hare and Hound was a pretty inn of white stone. However, the impression she received on the short walk through the yard was that it was not a thriving establishment. The innkeeper and his wife were elderly and appeared frail; certainly neither were capable of overpowering Sir Robert or the burly coachman in his hire. She could not involve these innocent people by throwing herself on their mercy and declaring that she was being abducted. Who knew what Sir Robert was capable of, if she pushed him too far.

Instead, she asked Sir Robert very politely if he might hire a private bedchamber so that she could perform her hasty toilette in pleasant surroundings.

Warily, he complied, but warned her that every moment lost meant Lottie was getting farther away.

Unfortunately, the elderly innkeeper led her not to a ground floor chamber, but up narrow creaking steps to a cozy room under the eaves. The bedchamber was neat and smelled faintly of lemon soap. Mary, relieved to be away from Sir Robert, rushed to secure the latch the moment the innkeeper's wife closed the door.

Short of his breaking through the wood, she was safe for the time being. She must seize these few moments to get away.

Her only means of escape appeared to be the short square window overlooking the sloping roof of an attached lean-to. Below was the back vegetable garden of the inn. At last, the years of physical work would be rewarded. She could squeeze through and get out onto the roof. Without a thought, she began to work the rusted window latch, stiff from years of neglect.

Whatever Sir Robert's plan, Mary was determined to thwart it!

At this moment Sir Robert was thinking that nothing could thwart his plans now. Rubbing his hands together, he smiled into his reflection in the polished brass hanging beside the fireplace in the inn parlor.

He really was quite a clever fellow. Mary may have been amazingly devious with Avalon, but she couldn't hold a candle to him.

She actually believed that they were going to the Thistle and Sword to save Lottie! What made it particularly amusing to his jaded sense of humor was that the Thistle and Sword was only a few miles farther up the pike. They would be passing it under cover of darkness and she'd never know. Mary would be wed at Gretna Green, just like her mother, before she realized what was happening. Then he'd have that unending source of wealth to tap.

He looked up sharply at the clatter of wheels in the yard. But he relaxed just as quickly. No one could possibly be after them.

The parlor door crashed open. A young man with huge eyes flashing in a set face stormed into the room with the beauteous Lady Arabella Hampton at his side.

"What have you done with Miss Masterton, you dastard!" he demanded, striding forward.

"I beg your pardon?" Sir Robert drawled with cool disdain, rapidly calculating the best course of action in the unforeseen turn of events. "Who the devil are you, and how dare you speak to me in that tone?"

"I am Lord Frederick Charlesworth, and I demand to see Miss Masterton at once. We've come to take her back to Avalon House."

Gauging the width of Charlesworth shoulders, Sir Robert shrugged. "I am accompanying Miss Masterton home to Hexham."

"You aren't accompanying Miss Masterton another step. If she wishes to return to Hexham, Avalon will see to it himself."

My God, the cocky pup even sounded like that devil! Refusing to acknowledge a slight tinge of apprehension, Robert sneered.

"Avalon has nothing to say concerning Miss Masterton's comings and goings."

"We'll see about that. I sent word back to him when we spied you forcing Mary into your carriage. He can't be far behind."

Now the apprehension burst into anger and frustration that anyone should dare attempt to ruin his plans, so close to fruition! Giving Charlesworth a look of contempt, he stepped past him, moving toward the door where Lady Arabella stood, her magnificent eyes wide in fear.

"You, sir, are staying here to answer to Avalon!" Charlesworth insisted putting a restraining hand on Robert's shoulder.

He whirled and, catching the boy off guard, was able to plan a facer on his jaw.

Lady Arabella's shrill scream echoed in the room as Charlesworth crumpled to the carpet.

"You monster!" she ranted, pushing past him to kneel in all her finery beside Charlesworth's limp form. "My darling, Frederick, speak to me," she sobbed, cradling his head in her lap.

Slightly off-balance from the turn of events, Sir Robert wasted precious moments watching Lady Arabella, beautiful even with tears reddening her cheeks, press kisses across Charlesworth's pale face.

Finally coming to his senses, he realized that it would behoove him to fetch Mary and get on with their journey. He turned toward the door and halted, blinking his eyes in disbelief. The Duchess of Avalon had arrived.

This was a whole different kind of adversary, but if he were clever, he might still pull it off. He made her a courtly bow. She ignored him to gaze at the tableau of the ton's reigning beauty clasping a man, not her betrothed, to her heaving bosom.

"Oh, Your Grace, that monster struck my brave Frederick without warning! What shall I do?" Arabella questioned, raising tear-washed eyes.

"It appears Frederick will do quite well himself," the duchess responded practically.

A loud moan from Charlesworth sent Lady Arabella into raptures. Again she covered his bruised cheek with kisses.

While the duchess seemed engrossed in the other occupants, Sir Robert attempted to sneak from the room.

"It would appear, Sir Robert, you have a deal to answer for." The duchess barely breathed the words, but they were enough to bring him up short.

Always a master at hiding his feelings, even under dire circumstances such as these, he gave her a polite smile. "I answer to no one. Not even the Duchess of Avalon."

"I believe, sir, you *will* answer to my son."

Admiration for her coolness warred with his need to make his escape. "However, your son is not here. Alas, by the time he arrives, Mary and I shall be long gone."

"You once accused me of appearing at the most inopportune moments. It appears I have done so again."

Avalon's hated drawl filled the room. Sir Robert had nowhere to run. Turning slowly, he stared into dark eyes filled with murder.

Chapter 13

There was some measure of satisfaction in seeing shock overcome the ever cool and calm Lancaster. His eyes went totally blank, then turned into two dark, unreadable hollows.

Richard gave a short, sharp laugh. "As my mother said, you have much to answer for, Lancaster. Where's Mary?"

Lifting one dark eyebrow, Sir Robert clasped his hands behind his back in a posture of relaxed congeniality. A smile lit the murky depths of his eyes. "Mary is no longer your concern. Nor has she ever been. Your true fiancée is the one clutching your . . . friend to her bosom."

Richard was fully aware of the scene taking place before the hearth. Frederick had managed to sit up, holding his swelling jaw in one palm, while Bella hovered over him like a mother hen. Actually she had never looked more beautiful. Great affection transformed one—a truth he'd recently discovered for himself.

He strode into the room determined to put an end to all the deception being practiced.

"We'll end this nonsense now, Lancaster!" His voice dropped to a menacing growl. "Your days of being Renfrew's minion are at an end. He was playing too deep, and the waters have closed over his head. You'll find the baron is leaving London. Permanently! Mary's fortune will be returned to her, and I can assure you, whatever he promised you for continuing to do his dirty work won't be forthcoming. You're finished!"

A mask of absolute calm slid over Sir Robert's face as he shrugged. "The accuracy of your perception must be a source of delight to your family and friends, Avalon. However, I don't know what it has to do with me. I know nothing of Mary's lost fortune or of her grandfather's actions. I am merely escorting her to find Miss Barton."

"What rubbish!" exclaimed Bella from her place at Charlesworth's side. "When Frederick attempted to restrain that man, he struck him without warning. Hardly the honorable actions of someone with nothing to hide!"

"Nicely spoken, Bella," Richard complimented. "As you can see, Lancaster, we *all* recognize your protestations as rubbish."

Sir Robert looked around the room frantically. He took two steps away from Richard's challenging stance, only to find himself hemmed in by Charlesworth, who had recovered sufficiently to be standing upright and was hell-bent for revenge.

"I know when to cut my losses," Lancaster admitted, rocking back slightly on his heels. "So the game is over. I will leave peacefully, Avalon. The field is yours."

"Not quite yet," Richard drawled coolly, stepping into the center of the room. With great pleasure he swung a powerful right cross into Lancaster's face.

Sir Robert toppled backward, overturning a small

pedestal table, and sending a pewter plate crashing to the floor to roll into the far corner.

"Now the game is over," Richard growled. Stepping over him, he extended his hand to Charlesworth. "Are you all right?" he asked with true affection.

"Should have seen it coming," Frederick muttered, looking decidedly sheepish.

"You did well." He clasped his shoulder and looked steadily into the enormously kind eyes. "You shall have your just reward."

Richard's gaze shifted to Bella's pale face. "I will leave it to you to send the notice of our broken engagement to *The Times*, Bella. And may I be the first to wish you both much happiness."

"No, Long! I can't let—" Frederick's noble protests were abruptly halted when Bella ruthlessly placed a full kiss upon his lips.

Satisfied, Richard turned to find his mother watching him, lights of pleasure and pride bursting forth in her eyes. "I believe you also have met your match, my dear."

He pressed a kiss on her soft scented cheek. "I've found what I was seeking. Or almost." He laughed a pure rich sound, free of constraint. "Where is she?

"Where is she?" he repeated in a harder voice, flicking a cold glance to where Sir Robert sprawled on the floor, blinking up at the ceiling. "I said, what have you done with Mary?" He bit the words out, striding over to straddle Lancaster's body.

Robert struggled up on his elbows, sneering. "Find the little baggage yourself!"

Goaded beyond bearing, Richard lunged downward and pulled Sir Robert to his feet, then shook him until his teeth rattled. "I'm not usually a violent man. However, it would be wise for you to push me no further!"

At last the calm façade cracked. Sir Robert's face split into cowardly fragments. "Don't hit me again! She's upstairs," he whined through colorless trembling lips.

Richard flung him away and raced out of the room, taking the narrow steps two at a time. The only door on the tiny landing was locked. He smiled at Mary's resourcefulness. He knocked gently.

"Mary, it's all right now. It's Avalon. I've come to take you home."

There was no answer.

The silence stretched to a full minute. He struck the wood harder.

"Mary, open the door. It's Avalon."

His temper was getting the better of him! He fleetingly thought of the old days when nothing and no one was able to flummox him. He banged his fist on the door again.

"Mary, open this damn door!"

Curling like a viper in his chest was the sudden unbelievable notion that Lancaster had harmed her in some way. Or spirited her away. With a roar of anguish he rammed his shoulder against the wood. The door shuddered but remained fast.

He took two steps back and lunged again. With a loud crack the lock gave way, and he stumbled over the threshold into the tiny room.

Swaying upright, he flashed an anxious glance around. Mary wasn't here, and there was no sign that she ever had been. Panic began to overtake him. He'd kill Lancaster if anything happened to Mary!

Then he noticed the curtain flutter at the open window. He crossed the room in two steps.

A steely coldness crept into his stomach at the sight of Mary dangling off the roof by her fingertips. He didn't dare call out for fear of startling her and causing her to lose her grip.

Sending a barrage of prayers heavenward, he stormed down the steps and raced toward the inn's kitchen garden.

The very first time he'd seen her she was risking her life to save her livestock. Now she was escaping her kidnapper by defying the danger of the rooftops! Was there ever such a woman before?

Standing just beneath her dangling slippers, he finally faced the truth. And in that moment he embraced it joyously.

There was only one Mary. And she would be his!

Dangling from the roof by trembling fingers Mary was forced to admit that, as an escape attempt, this ranked a miserable choice. She had sadly misjudged the distance to the rhubarb patch beneath her. Surely the plants would break her fall somewhat. Resigned to the fact that she had no recourse but to see this through, she closed her eyes and willed her fingers to release their frantic grip.

Suddenly a pair of arms grasped her.

Lancaster!

She let go and gave one desperate scream, struggling and kicking as she was swung through the air and set down among the carrots.

"Unhand me!" she cried, pounding a strong chest with her fists.

"Careful, Mary, you practically bowled me over!" With a mixture of joy and bewilderment she recognized Richard's lazy drawl. Stepping back, she brushed her hair out of her eyes and looked up at him.

This was not the same man who had stormed out of the parlor this morning. There was no anger, no confusion, no vulnerability in this face—just a smile of such warmth and power, heat washed through her trembling limbs.

"How did you find me?" she blurted out in confusion.

He reached out a well-shaped hand to cup her chin. "I've come to rescue you. And take you home."

She hardened her face, lifted her chin sharply out of his reach, and stepped back one pace.

"As you can see, I was rescuing myself. And I am going home—my home. After I fetch Lottie from the Thistle and Sword."

"There is something I need to tell you first. Afterward I will take you wherever you wish to go."

"If it's an apology for the dreadful things you said this morning you can just . . ." Her anger trailed away as she realized he'd come after her.

"I believe there are two apologies forthcoming. If my memory serves, you insulted me tit for tat." He stroked his cheek and his mouth twisted in a small half smile.

Bitter tears for all the lies that lay between them burned her eyes. Would she never learn? "It would seem we have both said more than enough to each other. There's nothing more. I'm going to find Lottie and return to Hexham where I belong."

Sparks struck in his dark eyes. He caught her wrist in a grip of steel. "Maybe it would be best for Lottie to be present when I tell you what I must. Come!"

She twisted her wrist uselessly within the trap of his fingers. "Where are you taking me?" she sobbed in frustration, running to keep up with his relentless pace.

"The Thistle and Sword!"

He tossed her up before him on Wildfire and clattered out of the inn yard. They traveled with such speed that the wind tore at her hair, whipping it wildly across her face, blinding her. Disoriented and frightened, she would have tumbled headfirst over Wildfire's flying mane if Richard hadn't kept her firmly secured against his chest, one arm low and intimate across her stomach.

The air whistled past so loudly it was impossible to speak, impossible to think of what she should do next.

In a remarkably short time she spied another inn, with a hanging sign proclaiming it the Thistle and Sword.

The instant Richard reined Wildfire to a halt, he released her. She slid out of his arms and off the horse with no help. After flinging him one withering look she rushed inside.

The taproom was shuttered. It took a moment for her eyes to adjust to the dark. If she had been the type of female prone to the vapors, she might have succumbed at that moment.

Lottie was clasped in her uncle's arms, pressing a fully reciprocated kiss onto his lips.

Mary tried to back out the way she'd come but was stopped by gentle hands on her shoulders. Richard cleared his throat pointedly.

Finally breaking free of his passionate embrace, Ian glanced up and saw them hovering in the doorway.

"Mary my girl! And Avalon! Wish us happy. Lottie and I are off to Gretna to be wed!" Ian's fiery beard split in a wide happy grin.

"Uncle Ian, how did you get my message so quickly?" Mary gasped, grateful for Richard's steadying presence. Her head was swimming. "It couldn't have possibly reached you in Hexham."

"Wasn't in Hexham. I was on this very pike, making my way to London because of your first letter. When I spied Avalon's insignia, I stopped the messenger."

Lottie positively cooed, standing in the haven of his arms. "He was coming to fetch me home."

Mary's eyes filled with tears. At least some happiness could come from this.

"Is there somewhere more private we can talk, Ian? I have a matter of great importance to impart to all of you."

Something in Richard's voice made Mary step hastily out of his range. Lottie indicated a narrow door.

"Here, Richard. We can use the private parlor."

The room was small, and the fire in the grate warmed the chill spreading through her. What else could Richard want? A great tiredness crept over her. If she could just go home, by herself, she was sure that in time she'd be back to normal.

But if she had to face him, or go back to London, she would never recover.

She turned to face him, to plead for mercy.

He stood in the middle of the room, his legs braced apart. A strange energy emanated from him, and his chocolate eyes melted over her with liquid warmth.

"Mary, this will no doubt come as a shock. So I'll tell you straight out. You're a great heiress."

"What?"

"Your grandmother's cousin amassed a great fortune in the colonies. When she died five years ago, she left it to your mother. Your grandfather has been keeping it for himself. I have made certain that it will come to you, where it belongs."

A great wash of anger surged over her, and she caught the back of an armchair to steady her knees. "Do you mean my parents could have seen their dream come true before they died?"

"Yes, Mary." He held up a hand when she tried to speak. "Don't worry. The old baron will pay. I made him promise to stay away from you and from London. He'll be forced to sell all those *things* he's been collecting with your money."

Her anger ebbed away, and she looked at Richard wonderingly.

"Now you can do anything you wish." Richard laughed, a rare true note that wiped all the cynicism from his face and left her gasping at his beauty. "However, at this precise moment I believe we must send the happy couple off on their elopement."

She was trembling, her thoughts capering like leaves before an autumn wind. She couldn't miss the long look that passed between Richard and her uncle before she was engulfed in Ian's powerful hug.

A moment later, Lottie's tear-streaked face was wreathed in a smile, for Ian pulled her back into his embrace and said, "We're all goin' to be happy, Mary my girl. See if we aren't." Then he whisked his blushing, blissful bride through the door.

She forced herself to be calm; whatever had happened in the past, some good was coming of it. There was no use holding on to an impossible dream.

"What will you do, Mary? You can do anything, you know. Stock the finest horse farm in all England. Or stay in London and take the ton by storm."

Mary lifted her chin, resolutely ignoring the flutterings in her stomach as he stepped closer.

"It was always my parents' dream to have the horse farm be successful. I must fulfill the dream for them," she answered as honestly as she could.

"Why must *you* fulfill it?" His voice was laced with such tenderness that she moved back a step from its undeniable appeal.

"Because it vindicates the choices they made," she whispered through the tears choking her throat. "For my mother to leave her world. For them to be together. For all they endured because of my grandfather's tryanny."

"But what of you, Mary? Of *your* dreams? Your grandfather has no power over you any longer. Surely you never accepted the ravings of that cruel heartless man. You belong wherever you choose to be. Only you can make that choice. What do *you* wish to do now?"

She half turned away from him, for fear he'd see her real wish in her eyes. Then she felt his breath at the back of her neck, and a searing finger of flame devoured her.

"Do you remember once telling me you hadn't known you were lonely until I came? Was that the truth?" The harsh urgency in his voice spun her around, practically into his arms. There was no place to retreat from him, with the fireplace at her back.

Truth and lies. Half lies and half truths. All that lay between them quivered in the air. If she could go back and change one moment of their time together, would she? Hadn't he brought her to this moment? Wasn't she much stronger, more resilient because of him?

The truth would leave her exposed before him. Once, she wouldn't have had the self-confidence to brave that moment. Now it was possible to meet and hold his gaze.

"Yes, I meant it. You . . . you made me feel, and grow inside. I'm sorry I lied to you about the engagement." Her voice gained strength. "But I'm not sorry for the moments we've shared."

Slowly he lifted her right hand, kissed the inside of her wrist, and laid her palm against the cheek she'd slapped that morning.

"I'm not sorry for any moments we've shared." His arms closed around her, and he brought his lips to within an inch of hers. "Will you kiss me, Mary?"

It was too much to resist, and always would be; his touch was as beguiling as his voice.

Raising her face, she met his lips eagerly. She shivered as his fingertips traced a slow, intricate pattern on her throat.

He pressed her closer, muttering endearments onto her cheeks, her eyes, the curve of her neck, and again on her eager mouth.

"Stay with me, Mary. There's no pretence in the way we touch each other," he whispered into her hair.

She was transported by the feelings of pleasure only he could inspire. For a moment she allowed herself the luxury of hope . . . until it was shattered by an equally strong reaction of guilt.

She pushed herself as far out of his arms as she could. That amounted to pressing her palms against his chest and making him look into her eyes, for he wouldn't let her go.

"But you are betrothed to Arabella!"

"If you'd seen Bella kissing Charlesworth, you would know my engagement is off. At this very moment they are no doubt discussing wedding plans with my mother back at the Hare and Hound."

Obviously her confusion was mirrored on her face, for he chuckled deep in his throat.

"Bella and Frederick saw Sir Robert take you up in his coach. They followed, but Freddie had the presence of mind to send a message back to Avalon House. My mother followed them, and I followed her. By the time I arrived, Lancaster had landed Charlesworth a facer and Bella was weeping all over him, displaying an overwhelming and undeniable affection."

"What happened to Sir Robert?" she asked, her head swimming again with the news of all these unforeseen, but much hoped–for, events.

"Rest assured he won't be bothering us again. I fear I became violent," he drawled with obvious satisfaction.

"I'm glad," she sighed, resting her cheek contentedly against his fine lawn shirt.

She felt the heat of his skin and was aware in new, exciting ways how their bodies touched and knitted one to the other.

He licked at her ear, slowly tracing its shape. "I love you, my bloodthirsty Mary. Dare I hope the sentiment might be returned?"

The pattern of her breathing changed. She tilted her head back to gaze up at him.

Vulnerability flickered behind his blazing eyes.

The expression on his proud face tore at her heart. Surely he couldn't doubt her response.

"I've loved you nearly from the beginning," she spoke in a voice rich with feeling. "Perhaps . . . perhaps I could finance the horse farm for Uncle Ian and Lottie. Then I could stay in London. We . . . we could be together."

His husky laugh caressed her face, as his fingers tangled gently in her hair. "My sweet life, it doesn't matter where you choose to be. I'll follow."

"You'd do that for me?" she whispered.

Their eyes found each other, the meeting achingly sweet, full of promise for the future.

"I would do it for the same reason your mother followed her heart—the same reason she was content with her choice. It doesn't matter where I am, as long as I'm with you."

Mary believed him.

More Romance
from Regency